Windflower Fugue

Martha Lee

To Virginia Sweetser,
who championed this story
from the beginning.

To Nancy –
With my
very best wishes.
Martha Lee
October, 2013

PART I

Something sharp and shiny sticking out of the sand caught Helmi's eye as she ambled down the beach. Stooping to inspect the tiny shaft tossing sun-rays off its scalloped sides, she could not believe her luck. Always in search of an arrowhead, she ordained this one a good omen. A five-inch, reddish piece of chiseled jasper or cinnabar, it leaned north as if pointing the way.

She took the cue, continuing on her course. Periodically she reached into her pocket to rub the rough relic as if it were endowed with magic powers. It could be a key factor in helping her find the farm at the end of her relentless pilgrimage.

None of the places she had seen so far was suitable enough. Above all she craved peace, a place where her spirit could soar, her work flourish. A cramped little plot would never do. She envisioned a great patch of land - acres of woods, a sparkling stream, even an orchard - spreading down to the sea. And amidst this gentle idyll the old house, skirted by a split-rail porch, would secretly repose.

To crown things, an abandoned barn would sit down the road a little way beyond the house. She would convert part of it into a studio, board her horse in the rest, garden in the orchard and build roaring fires in the house.

She was beginning to believe what people had been telling her for years: that she would never find a small farm on the ocean - no such thing existed. Oh, they said, she might find a few acres with trees, possibly even with a creek, but it wouldn't be oceanfront - no such thing existed. Or she might find some ocean frontage with trees and a creek but it wouldn't have a house and barn on it - no such thing existed. So far she'd looked at dozens of listings and so far they'd been right - no such thing existed.

Somehow today she felt something different - like this could be her lucky day. Groping inside her pocket again, she lightly touched the arrowhead. She had just about reached the spot up the coast where it had pointed. Wild sea grass densely thicketed the high, rolling dunes, hiding from the shore what lay beyond.

She walked along the crest of the dunes for what seemed a long stretch, all the while studying the sparse patches of small beach cottages lining the flatlands. Each one was barely visible through the tall grasses growing rampant near their bases. Occasionally a smoke spiral curled from a chimney stack marking the only hint of a homestead.

Between the hump-backed dunes she spied a path of softly-trod sea grass stretching toward the horizon. She could not tell if it led anywhere particular but something compelling about its meandering retreat piqued her curiosity. Almost against her will she felt pulled along its soft, cushiony length. Unlike some of the other paths, this one's far end was obscured by a broad stand of evergreens.

Forging through thick underbrush and giant timber she came out onto a large, circular clearing. At its heart a log structure stood resembling a hunting lodge in miniature. Soon she was pressing her nose up against one of its small, wood-framed panes. She caught her breath at the sight.

Inside it was so cool, so dark and mysterious. So dark she could barely distinguish the separate rooms and sparsely scattered furnishings. Several of the chairs and tables looked hand-hewn. The walls were mortar-embedded logs thickly varnished to a rich patina. Floors were the same deep aged-pine hue, though even heavy polish didn't obscure intricately-veined scarring by scratches and gouges. A massive counter-bar was tucked into the left-hand corner of the front room. Helmi could barely discern the contents of the large, open room beyond except for one edge of what looked to be a hearth and stone-encrusted fireplace. The forms of everything else were shrouded in shadows. A tattered, faded rug rested under spindle-legged chairs. A wide porch almost completely encircled the cabin off which the front and back doors opened into the house. The weathered shake roof was thickly padded with moss. It would have been extremely austere were it not for the warm-toned wood and subtly-colored scatter rugs.

There was no sign of life. She could not see any personal affects or touches to do with daily living. There was not a flower, a shoe or sock, pot or pan, not one thing to indicate human habitation. She vowed to find out who owned it, what it was used for, if it was for sale or lease. If it could be had, she would have it.

She took a trail along the side of the house leading through a clump of trees and bushes. It reminded her of an ancient rainforest. Some of the tree trunks looked nearly twenty feet thick. Along the way she spotted a primeval-like pond alive with goldfish, tadpoles, frogs and water lilies. Its weed and algae-infested waters charmed her. Even they were major food chain sources.

Further down the path she came to a woodshed stacked ceiling-high with logs and kindling. Chopping sounds drew her round back of the lean-to. The sudden sight of a man, ax poised in mid-air ready to strike, brought her up sharply. Though also startled he rendered a swift whack to the piece perched on a stump just as it splintered loudly in two.

He had the dark, wild eyes and olive skin of a gypsy, yet a jutting jaw, beaked nose and thick henna-color hair made him look more like a Macaw warrior. He wasn't much taller than Helmi, but his proportions, including massive shoulders and hands, were powerful. Buckskin breeches and a chamois shirt strengthened further the impact of that first impression.

He seemed barely to notice her, scarcely aware of her presence, maintaining a rhythmic pace to his chopping. He seemed to be pretending she wasn't there, willing her to leave. Rooted where she stood like a pillar of stone, her limbs had petrified. Lead weights. No matter how hard she tried to move, they wouldn't budge.

Finally she figured it wasn't her he minded so much as the distasteful prospect of speaking.

We're alike that way, she thought.

After tossing a good-sized load into a wheelbarrow he headed down the path to the main house. She decided to follow but from a decent distance so as not to provoke him.

At the rear of the cabin he dumped the wood out and stacked

it on top of an existing pile, then turned back toward the shed.

Risking looking like a lost puppy, she trailed after him. She didn't care. She had to find out who he was, where he came from, whether he was living at the cabin, renting it or merely working there and if so, who employed him.

This time when he got back to the shed, instead of resuming his chopping he disappeared behind the building. Just as she arrived, he vanished through the door of a tiny glass annex that resembled a greenhouse.

Up closer, peering through the panes, she could make out rows of wood work tables covered with clay pots filled with plants and flowers. Taller shrubs and small trees stood on the dirt floor and everywhere there were billowing hanging baskets, vine-covered trellises and lattice supports.

It was an exquisite little hothouse, full of steamy exoticism, the sun searing down through glass roof panes. Everything was glass, even the doors. Humidity from the solar heat caused the windows to fog up, making them look frosted. It had very simple, basic structural lines yet its solid, careful construction aspired toward the classical.

She could barely distinguish the plants inside, but saw a blurry mix of hibiscus, orchids, roses, begonias and jasmine. Baskets of fuchsias and ivy geraniums draped down over them. Ficus and palm trees formed narrow allées along the aisles.

The stranger seemed startled when he noticed her peering in at him, but kept on stuffing soil into different pots, gently stirring it around the roots of new shoots. Again he became deeply immersed in his task, totally ignoring her. His features softened into beatific repose. Elbow-deep in dirt it was obvious that connecting with the earth was direly important to him. She envied his ecstasy as soil seeped into his skin like an organic transfusion. She craved its cool moistness, revered its life-sustaining matter. Without it she knew her spirit could not survive.

Knute Corsun emerged from the greenhouse and set off for the far pasture. He was still puzzling over the mysterious woman stalking him when he reached the fence. It was time to tend the horses, chores he could perform by rote and still pursue the question of his uninvited guest.

He swung the old wooden gate open and sauntered toward

the small herd of horses grazing near a stand of hemlocks. His heart always jumped whenever he set eyes on their wild beauty.

They're free spirits alright.
They're still so untamed they hardly let
me near them. If it weren't for their
food and water, they wouldn't have
anything to do with me.

He'd rounded them up himself on state land in eastern Oregon. The Bureau of Land Management, sponsor of a program to stabilize the wild horse population, had hired him to capture the little band and transport them to a large tract of land it owned in neighboring Washington state *No small job*, he mused, remembering the daunting feat of lassoing a wild stallion galloping across fifty five hundred acres of land going thirty five miles an hour. It had taken him three days to gather up the ten he'd set his sights on. Then days more to haul them, in separate groups, to their new home.

Helmi, camouflaged in the shrubbery while taking in the scene, was awestruck. The sight of ten beauteous creatures, their powerful necks arched gracefully as they nibbled thick marsh grass, was magical. She'd never before seen horses like these. They were like ballerinas, strong yet lithe. Their pale ochre bodies were framed by dark brown manes, tails and stockings. Zebra stripes zigzagged down their front legs. Their shapely heads were huge with black noses and dark, pointed ears. They whinnied alert signals as Knute approached, reminding Helmi of an Hovaness symphony.

Instinctively, as they rose up and back skittishly, cloaked in ethereal mystery, she knew that they were the wildest, most primitive spirits she had ever seen.

One of the stallions tossed his head, frenziedly pawing the ground, as he caught her scent. She was desperate to get nearer but decided instead to lay in wait for some sign from the man. Again he seemed oblivious of her as he carried an armload of hay from the barn to a wooden feed stand. A large trough of water stood nearby. The horses steered clear of him, skirting a wide area until he backed away. Slowly they approached the food, alert and cautious.

Helmi, hidden in the bushes, stood watching them feed for a

long time. She felt sublimely peaceful and content and, at that moment, would rather be there with them than anywhere else on earth. They were her friends, her protectors, her soul mates. She was one with them like she never could be with humans. To her, they were human. She must think up fitting names for each of them. But first she needed to learn their inner workings, their strength and foibles, likes and dislikes, habits and tastes. It might take some time. If only the man would accept her, let her work with him, maybe find things she could do to help.

Since discovering the farm she knew she could not go back. Her boarding house was just down the beach but she would not return except to pick up her few possessions. Nothing was back there for her. Things had changed dramatically and forever. She was determined to stay at the farm even if it meant sleeping in the barn.

The horses had finished their meal. Some started out for the far pasture. But her attention was focused on the big stallion. He was heading for the barn and since that would probably be her new home for awhile she decided to follow, curious to find out what it was like.

It was tucked away in the midst of a small patch of shore pines at one end of the inner pasture. Long and narrow with weathered gray cedar board-and-batten siding, its roof angled up on either side to the arched top. Five shuttered stall windows opened out along the outer walls.

Helmi went inside through the wide double doors at the south end. Once her eyes adjusted to the dim light she noticed, to her left, a storeroom piled high with thick hay bales. She peeked through the door to the right and saw a neatly outfitted tack room. Several saddles and bridles hung from wooden pegs lining the wall. A huge old roll-top desk stuffed with books and papers sat in the corner. Several framed, antique English hunting prints livened the wood-paneled walls and rush matting covered the floor.

The barn's long, dirt-covered center aisle led between the stalls to the double doors at the far end.

Helmi heard some muffled shuffling toward the end of the aisle and went to investigate.

She found the stallion there munching contentedly away at hay stuffed inside a feed bin tacked to the wall.

She clung to the stall gate for a long while, unable to wrench her gaze from the winsome steed. He was more exquisite than anything she remembered ever having seen before.

He was not easy with strangers. As Helmi neared he wheeled in the stall to face her. His dark, heavy-lidded eyes cast a wild sheen as he stared into her own. Snorting nervously he flared his nostrils and stomped the ground as if warning her to keep her distance. Before he could back away she reached instinctively up to stroke his face. He shied as if stung. She saw he was intrigued by her, sensing she was a kindred spirit. Inching closer he caught her scent. She answered by sniffing into his nostrils Indian fashion. He responded this time by standing in place when she touched the soft velvet blackness of his nose. Gently she stroked the muscular length of his neck beneath the wiry black mane.

She was studying his every detail so intently that she did not notice the man approach. So quietly he appeared that his presence seemed more like an apparition. There he was staring with her up at the great stallion. This time there was no uneasiness. The horse seemed conscious of a certain bond of communion with the man. There was no reluctance, no hesitation. He knew the man and there was trust between them. It was no easy affection they shared, but rather a kind of guarded respect. Instantaneously the three untamed hearts linked in silent bondage, like the unanimous consensus in some private rite.

She sensed a mysterious force emanating from the man, felt a heat stirring from his being. His scent, a mingle of hay, horse and sweat, rose in her nostrils like a spiral of wood smoke. Sweet and sour at the same time. A bittersweet reminder of other times, other places. Flashes of overwhelming warmth flooded through her and when their arms touched she shied away as if scalded.

His glance at her was a startled mix of curiosity and indifference. His eyes looked momentarily bemused, then too busy to be bothered pursuing it.

He grabbed the lead rope, snapped it to the halter and pulled the dun out of his stall.

Helmi watched as he deftly saddled and bridled him, then walked him down the hallway and out into the pasture.

Horse and rider both turned back to give her a parting stare, then shot out toward the trail leading into the woods.

She moodily sniffed the musty smells of horse flesh and stale dung left clinging in their wake.

Dejectedly she sidled over to the other stalls and discovered one holding a stunning Appaloosa splattered with tiny paint-like spots. She was instantly smitten and felt much less alone.

The lithesome mare nuzzled her cheek and snorted a greeting into her nose. She seemed to crave affection, echoing Helmi's own desires like a distant fugue.

She picked up the lead rope hanging on a nail beside the stall, hooked it onto the halter and nudged her gently out.

She got no resistance, only a perfect willingness to comply.

They walked back and forth down the center aisle in complete accord over and over for a long time, all the while communing silently, deeply.

You are exquisite. Where have you come from? Who do you belong to? No. I know better than that. No one could ever truly own you. Not such wild beauty as yours. It will always remain untamed, must always be free, unbound, utterly independent. To me you are the embodiment of liberty defiant against the will. We may only partake of your mystique from a distance, keep you unfettered, honor your native heritage. But will you at least be my friend? Might you permit me to be yours?

The lovely mare whinnied softly, tossing her noble head up and down as if nodding in assent.

There was something disarmingly wise aglow in the soft, liquid brown of her eyes. She seemed uncommonly learned beyond her years. Yet there was a sparkle to her gaze, a spring to her step belying her wisdom and lending a magical aura to her presence.

What is your name I wonder? What do they call you? I must think of some special name that suits your wild beauty, your grace, your proud spirit and omniscience. What would you wish to be called? I shall give it a great deal of consideration before letting you in on what I've come up with. It must capture the rebel in your soul, the poetry in your stride, your soaring heart. It will come to me. The absolute perfect one will appear to me soon.....

The mare offered no resistance to the impassioned pronouncement, but instead seemed to accept it as destiny. A name of her own, or the lack of one, seemed of no special import to her or affect her one way or the other. She was poised, confident and comfortable enough within herself without the baggage which might come with some given label.

But it was most important to Helmi who attached great significance to names. They were not merely monikers but, on a deeper level, symbols connecting an entity with the spirit world, linking it with ancient properties inherited from primeval times and predecessors. Names signified the prelude to one's destiny, the first step in the odyssey toward some eventual wholeness.

There is a great deal in a name, yes. Much more than merely its look, sound or rhythm. It may be the key that unlocks the mysteries of one's existence.

All of a sudden it's dawned on me. I will call you Windflower. It is another name for a rare flower that lives near the sea. Your beauty not only matches but surmounts that of a field of wild sea anemones. There are certain spots around here where they are said to be found. I believe it is so and will continue my search. Someday we will ride together through a meadow filled with them.

The mare suddenly danced excitedly about as if to second the motion. The matter was settled. She seemed extremely pleased with her brand new appellation.

Windflower.   Windflower.
Windflower. You do seem to relish it
and how it suits you.   It will be our
little secret.   No one else need ever
know.

And the mare's short staccato whinnies echoed through the stall chambers in resounding concurrence.

Soon they heard the shuffling noise of tall grasses being trampled in the distance.

"Quick now, he's coming back," Helmi whispered to Windflower as she guided her into her stall, released her and replaced the lead rope.

She let out a sigh of relief. Glancing around nothing looked out of place but just as he had left it.

Still, something was not quite right.   And then she remembered. Windflower's feed box had been on the left wall. Now it was on the right. Windflower was in the wrong stall. But too late. The man dismounted and entered the barn.

Several seconds later he picked out a small white oval from the dimness. Her dogged presence perturbed him. Her ghostly pallor puzzled him. Something shocking had happened but he wasn't baffled for long. The mare was not in her stall but next door. He acted like nothing was amiss, going about the business of getting the stallion ready to go in.

Helmi stood watching from the shadows as he pulled off the saddle and vigorously brushed him down.   Droplets of sweat misted the air. She knew from all the panting and snorting that wherever they had gone they had ridden hard. Probably along the beach from the looks of the dun's sand-encrusted legs and hooves. Impatient jabs at the ground made it clear he did not relish being groomed. He danced sideways then back and forth trying to get clear of the bristly stroking.

Many more sessions before the embedded grit of countless runs was shed.   An endless cycle of purging telltale signs; a ritualistic tug-of-war between master and charge.

"What went on here while I was gone?"

"I just wanted to see if I could get to know the Appy a bit better. She's beautiful and mysterious, but seemed desperately lonely so I decided to take her out for a little stroll."

"She's a feisty one. Won't usually let anyone near her without a ruckus. How'd you fare?"

"We got along like two long lost friends. She acted as if she knew me and seemed ecstatic with the attention."

Knute had stepped inside the stall and she skittishly sidestepped to avoid him. He rubbed his thick fingers over her back and sides in an effort to calm her, then led her over to her own stall.

"Easy girl," he droned in a steady monotone. "Nobody's going to hurt you. You're safe. Why so antsy? Need some exercise? Probably rather have a nice big dinner."

Helmi followed him into a small dark room smelling of cedar, green hay and grain. He scooped out a can full of pellets into a bucket, grabbed an armful of hay and headed back to the mare.

She sniffed expectantly, pulling out a mouthful of hay as he poured the feed into her bin. She scrambled for it with zeal, like one who hadn't eaten for days.

"She's always like that, " Knute responded to Helmi's unasked question. "They all are. Can't seem to get enough of it. No matter how much they get, it's never enough. Must be the alfalfa and molasses in it. Whatever it is, they're crazy for it. Never get tired of it. Always want more."

Helmi watched, amazed as Windflower pawed the dirt floor and devoured the pellets one by one. When she finished she started in on the mound of hay. Her rhythmic munching sounded to Helmi like someone chewing dill pickles.

As they headed out of the barn, Knute fished for information about the shadow-woman.

"Name's Knute Corsun."

She had been too absorbed to introduce herself.

"I'm Helmi Seaborne. I hope you don't mind my intruding. I was on a walk on the beach down from my boarding house, noticed your trail and couldn't help checking it out. I'm afraid my curiosity got the better of me."

"No great harm done," he said slowly in his low monotone. "You're on public property. This land is part of the Wiakiakum Preserve. The state hired me around five years ago. I'm in charge of the land, buildings and animals."

"I was afraid I might be trespassing. But what about the horses? Who do they belong to? I thought you owned them."

"In a way I do. I went after them in Oregon for the conservancy, rounded them up and brought them back here. They're part of a program to relocate wild herds that have outgrown their territory. It'll take decades before they've overrun this acreage. They belong to the state but since I've been tending them I forget sometimes and think they're mine. They might as well be. I'm about the only human they've ever known. Not that they could ever really belong to anyone."

"They're truly the most exquisite creatures I've ever seen," Helmi managed an awed whisper. Her strangled tone sounded as if coming from very deep down.

Knute eyed her intently as she spoke. Her voice was childlike with wonder, her eyes huge with amazement. He did not often come in contact with one so reactive. It caught him slightly off guard. Not just her excitement, but the intrigue she aroused. She definitely was a different stripe than he had ever encountered.

Too skinny. That's for sure. But, then again, she's tall so she carries it well, like some half-starved wild animal. Looks and acts more like a scared antelope or gazelle. She's surprised and mystified by things like an animal would be that's just emerged from the forest after a long hibernation. Her eyes and voice are soft and gentle as a doe. Her hair's rich and deep as Madrona bark, smells as sweet as spring grass. But way too boney. And skittish. Might need to be broken in a bit before she tames down. Not so's to break her spirit though.

He wondered if maybe she thought she was a horse. She did seem to have an uncanny rapport with the two she'd met, the stallion and the mare. He would not be surprised. He often thought he was more horse than human and would not mind if he were.

Mystery veiled her like mist rising from the falls. Her movements were stealthy like a stalking panther. She looked as though she lived in a secret garden - only she possessed the key - floating in and out as if in a dream.

Whatever he was thinking, fiercely he kept it to himself. He was stoic to an unnatural degree, not sharing even the tiniest morsel of himself with Helmi.

When he had finished feeding the horses, both in the field and barn, he started walking back to the cabin Helmi had, at first, thought was abandoned. On the way in he grabbed several logs and an armful of kindling to start the fire for the dinner hour.

"You're welcome to join me if you'd care to," he offered reluctantly. He was not used to strangers and did not especially relish their company. But she was odd, an unusual variety and a tad bit better to have around, though too snoopy.

Helmi, startled, at first, by his sudden hospitality, did not hesitate to accept. They walked together, in silence, up the road to the house.

With Helmi close behind him, he kicked the door open and went to the hearth to set the pile of wood down.

When she had first looked in she could not see what lay beyond the fireplace. Now she saw that a narrow set of wood steps, almost like a makeshift ladder, propped against the back wall, led up to a loft-like area above.

Helmi guessed he must sleep up there since she did not see anything to sleep on in the main great room, very little even to sit on, and no adjoining rooms that might be bedrooms.

A good size fire was soon crackling, ablaze on the iron grate. She stood before it to thaw her chilled limbs and damp clothes.

Knute went behind the counter and started opening and shutting cupboards. Soon she heard the familiar sounds of pans clattering, silverware rattling and glasses tinkling.

He quickly set the table, placing a dried arrangement and saggy candle in the center beside a large bottle of wine. Two chairs surfaced from unknown whereabouts. The place was beginning to look and feel almost cozy.

Savory aromas drifted their way through the room and Helmi, mellow from the fire, was enticed and ravenous.

There was plenty to sate her hearty appetite. They devoured

venison stew, corned-beef hash, russet potatoes and vegetable salad with vinaigrette dressing - all washed down with a robust claret. Helmi, incredulous at how good it all was, felt deliciously satisfied.

As the sun set and dusk descended the silhouettes of their faces glowed in the dimming candlelight.

"The venison was fabulous. Absolutely done to perfection. Where did you get it?" she asked, the flavor of wild game still sitting on her tongue.

"Each fall the warden allows me to bring down a few of the Roosevelt elk roaming these woods. Too many grazing at one time and they get to be a nuisance," he replied gruffly. "I quarter 'em myself into enough cuts to last the rest of the year."

"I've never eaten anything so delectable," she said with vehemence.

But the meal was not over yet. He still had tapioca pudding and fresh-ground coffee to serve. He could not have had a more appreciative guest than he did in Helmi.

He seemed bemused and buoyed by her obvious pleasure.

"You seem to have a facility for gourmet cooking," she continued in the same vein.

"Not really," he protested. "Just self-taught out of sheer necessity and a yen for edible food."

"That meal was far beyond edible. It was good enough to have been served in the poshest of restaurants," she countered.

"What's been your experience with eating in posh restaurants?" he challenged her, his curiosity seemingly genuine.

"I've been in quite a few here and there. And a few years ago I took my Grand Tour through Europe eating in some of its better places along the way. I rather fancy myself as somewhat of a gourmand. At least I've trained my palate to know an excellent meal when I'm eating it," she explained patiently, despite the nettlesome overtones of his query.

"I don't think I ever ate a bad meal in France," she added. "One of my favorite places was a lovely inn called the Chateau Jardin in Tours. Did you know Balzac lived in Tours? Anyway, I still remember the white linen, fresh roses and candlelight, being able to look out and see all the different greens in the manicured garden. I even remember what I ordered and how elegant it was -

fresh squid wrapped in grape leaves. I went back at least three times to try other things.

"Then there were the different kinds of patés, all prepared and served exquisitely at a small hotel in Dijon, just as an appetizer.

"And the bouillabaisse at a tiny seaside cafe with the blue and white striped awning at Juan-le-Pins where Picasso used to eat. Each layer of fresh fish was brought separately and served in a huge soup platter.

"Sampling a lot of the wines on my way through the Loire Valley where they were produced, was a special treat, too.

"I remember a delicious veal dish in the Soho section of London and especially the world-famous fettuccini at Alfredo's in Rome. Surprisingly no cream, just loads of sweet cream butter and parmesan.

"There were many more notable meals, too many to mention, but not to remember."

He looked preoccupied, almost as if he were chewing the contents of her monologue. She had humbled him into silence, it seemed, with her vast culinary experience.

She had so many things to ask him but thought better of it, afraid he might close up completely. She did not want to unnerve him with questions.

They pulled up their chairs in front of the fire to sip their coffee.

He sat and stared at the flames for a long while, preferring the silence to conversation.

She did not want to ruin the moment. The peace was heavenly. She decided she would bide her time until the day he might offer up something more of himself.

"I should be going. It's getting dark," she said.

"I'll walk you back if you like."

"Yes. I was hoping you would. It's not far."

They set off down the trail to the beach. The sky was clear - she thought she had never seen so many stars at one time - spangled with a billion sequins. A nearly full moon, shining over the whitecaps, silhouetted the sea birds.

They walked as close to the surf as possible without getting wet, slowly, silently; the sound of the waves, a fugue, plundering their thoughts.

About two miles down the beach they came to the pathway leading up to the lodge. It was a rambling wooden house with an octagonal, shingled steeple serving as the roof's centerpiece.

Lamplight, glowing from every window, lent it a warm, welcoming air.

On the veranda he stared deeply into her eyes a few moments, searching as if for hidden clues and then was gone.

She wanted to shout that she would be back, must be there again, but he had already vanished.

> *Such an ethereal spirit and what an ephemeral flow about the hours we spent together, more like a dream,* she whispered to herself. *A strange and mysterious creature. What is it about that man that I find so compelling?*

She climbed the broad staircase to her room and lay down on the old four-poster. Wrapping herself in the patchwork quilt, she fought against the sleep that was overtaking her. It would only be, as was the norm, another restless bout of tossing and turning. A night, for once, during which she did not wake up at least ten times would be so rare.

The smell of bacon and eggs floating up the stairs from the kitchen served as her alarm clock the next morning.

But even it was barely enough to stir her. Still so tired, unbelievably tired. The last thing she felt like doing was to get up. She had not slept at all well once again and doubted if she ever would. Going to bed was getting to be like a dreaded nightmare.

She straggled into the dining room. Most of the other lodgers had eaten and were already headed out for the day.

She had her usual loggers' breakfast of two fried eggs, country sausage, hash browns, toast and juice. Yet rather than revive her, it made her feel more sluggish.

She looked around the drafty old room. The old-fashioned flowered wallpaper was peeling in places. Still it had a somewhat homey charm. There was something comforting about its drab, gentile shabbiness. She felt almost at home and sank into an overstuffed chair in front of the fireplace. Never was she happier than sitting before a fire. She just could never seem to be warm enough. The heat of the flames reached out to engulf her like a lover's arms.

She felt the warmth and gave a slight shiver. *Will I see him again today?*

The true question was whether she would be able to muster the energy to make the effort.

She had not felt like working for a long time. She knew she must get back to it soon or the lost momentum would be too great to retrieve.

Her work, in past times, had always been her salvation, a panacea of sorts. A haven from the chaos, inside as well as out. Rarely safe but at least a familiar port where certain demons stayed at bay. Occasionally they crept into the work but she was usually able to exorcise them before the damage got to be too extensive.

> *Yes,* she thought, *it's nearly time to set up my studio again. I must work if I want to retain my senses. And my sanity. My spirit needs desperately to be recharged.*

She had temporarily lost her way but was determined to get back on track. She wished to soar, again, upward and inward. To feel, again, free and exhilarated. Taste, again, the salty flavor of passion and obsession. To know these things, again, was paramount for the elemental core of her essence to survive.

Body, mind and spirit - heal, she commanded over and over, hoping her innermost being could hear and was receptive. *Body, mind and spirit - heal, heal, please HEAL. Finally, once and for all, please, before it is too late. No, I'm not going to put rocks in my pockets and walk into the sea,* she mused. *But sometimes I have to kick myself to keep from thinking about doing just that.*

In the past years she had given up everything: husband, home, security, a legion of lovers. Sacrificed in order to strike out on her own, to shape her own destiny. Lost so that beneath crushing layers of burden, guilt, denial and duty, she could be found.

The sea, forever stable, forever stalwart, forever steadfast, her immortal companion. All else was in flux. No matter how tumultuous the surf, it would always return, to soothe, comfort and reassure. It would not vanish, but would be there forever, despite all else.

To be by the sea, live near it, walk by it, feel, hear and see it fueled her fantasies and touched her to the quick.

Everyday, combing the beach, she loosed the wellspring of her imaginings on dreams run rampant.

She unleashed her senses to soak up the thousands upon thousands of intricate patterns and delicate markings woven in the sand by birds, waves, sea foam. To study the shadow creations of the clouds reflected in the shore's glossy mirror. To breathe in the tangy scent of saltwater sprays tossed with seaweed. To feel the clammy mist permeating every pore and piece of clothing.

The sound of the sea, as she walked along the shore, played in the background like a distant fugue. Faint, then thunderous; mysterious echoes beckoning her to venture forth.

Gathering sand dollars to while away the time, her collection was growing. Her best harvest yet - thirty all tolled. Even after she put the living ones back. Not much luck finding anything more exotic. Once a large crab she stuffed into her clam gun and cooked for dinner. Hundreds of clams but no glass floats, no old bottles bearing messages from afar, not a single starfish. Still, she had the Midas touch with sand dollars - to find each time more than the last - seemed a good sign of sorts. Could such good fortune signal fortuitous aspects in her future? Superstition had a strange way of sneaking up on her so that momentarily she suspended disbelief. Possibilities loomed endlessly.

The forecast Arctic front began rolling in. Her hands and feet felt like chunks of ice. A bracing wind was picking up, making her ears ache and her eyes sting. Sand clouds swirled around her legs. The breakers swelled ominously. The sudden metamorphosis stunned her. Never had she known anyplace more temperamental or unpredictable.

But she did not run away, though soaked to the bone. The sea bewitched her no matter what the weather. The storm's wild beauty conjured a visual feast more satisfying than the choicest delicacy. Her soul thrived on it as if it were some great aphrodisiac.

Finally, after she was almost too chilled to move, she

trekked slowly back to her room. Even in the midst of a storm she was reluctant to leave. It seemed uncomfortably close to abandoning a loved one in trouble.

All the commotion on the beach left her feeling drained and unsettled inside. With her last ounce of strength she crept onto her bed, curled up catlike and fell deep into oblivion. She missed the dinner hour, sleeping straight through the night and well into the next day. It was nearly noon as she fought her way back to consciousness. The sun was streaming through the shutters, turning everything in the room to stripes. Through the slats she could see clouds floating by but they were no longer threatening. Patches of blue sky opened up between the fleecy whiteness of their huge pillow forms.

The biting cold of the night before still hung in the air causing her to burrow back under the covers. She felt equipped to survive virtually anything - even a scorching summer day in the desert - except being too cold. Nothing at that moment could be more taxing than getting out of bed. *My landlords must be economizing,* she thought in disgust. *There is no excuse for keeping a place so frigid, not even destitution.*

She would have to complain vehemently, a task she relished little more than battling freezing climate. Confrontations were not her forte unless under extreme duress. Provocation prompted her into certain actions otherwise against the grain.

She felt too frustrated to do much of anything. Bleak weather, loneliness and despair conspired to sabotage her. Every plan or effort she made was doomed from the start beginning with a heavy heart.

Incessant rain, pelting the roof, beat her down into a well of stupor causing her to wonder if she could ever climb out to see the light again.

She wandered into the main great room. Cedar walls, ebony-stained hardwood floors and beamed ceilings cast a shadowy mystery over numerous tables, chairs, scatter rugs and throws. Reflections from the floor and desk lamps' colored glass shades mingled with the firelight to exude a soft, rich glow. Magazines, books and newspapers sprawled over every surface and a stack of games and puzzles hovered in the corner. It was the kind of room she loved best, suffused with a shabby rusticity, inviting her to flop down anywhere, put up her feet and stretch out.

She pulled up an old Mission-style armchair, its seat padded with a faded Kilim, in front of the fire and opened her book.

It was an old custom. Whenever she spiraled into a slump she sought out her trusted companions, books, to keep her company at all hours, in all seasons, on all occasions. Between their covers resided the real world - labyrinthine excursions into Netherlands filled with poetry, mystery, even exquisite beauty.

Her toes were warming up. The warmth surged through her like a transfusion. The stiffness in her limbs was leaving as the pliancy of lifeblood seeped slowly in.

Soon she was lost in time, soon lost in space, lost in infinity. Losing all sense of time, place, the outside world, she sank further into the work before her, voraciously devouring great chunks, hungry as a starved animal.

The deeper she delved into the story, the more dramatically her spirits lifted. But so far had they plummeted that only drastic measures would resuscitate them. To throw off the pall that had plunged them into the abyss. Her home remedy was coming to the rescue and beginning to do its work. Her anguish was ebbing and with it the wretched knot of desolation was unraveling. Her salvation was managing, once again, to shake off the malaise.

Day by day she followed the same routine she had carved for herself. First a big breakfast, then rocking by the fire, journal-writing, reading long passages in her book, a walk on the beach, dinner, then early to bed.

And daily, by the fire, by the sea, reading or walking she threaded her way through the daydreams that bound her together. Dreams of the day she would take up her brushes again. Dreams of the paintings to come, envisioning them, what they might be, their hues, sizes and textures, the look of their lines and forms.

She would start again, small at first, like the beginning so long ago. Tiny pieces of linen layered with oil, etched with symbols, colored with shades of earth and elements. They would be the studies for a growing, organic series, her own very personal, gradually expanding, body of life-work.

Until that mythical day she would forge ahead in her quest for strength, for patience, for courage, for love. She would draw on the sea, the sand, the rocks, the stars, the trees for solace, for hope, for sustenance.

A sudden flash of insight told her it may be long in coming and so very much longer in the making.

The memory of Knute Corsun and Windflower constantly invaded her reveries. She surmised that the debilitating feeling of emptiness plaguing her was somehow linked with them. A strong urge for connectedness gripped her, almost palpably pushing her toward them. But, in the end, she balked. At the last minute she regained her senses and recouped her composure. It was still too premature to test the waters or brave the elemental forces of another romance. Any aspirations toward grand passion, no matter how fervidly anticipated must be postponed indefinitely. Too many doubts and fears remained to be conquered. And though she took pride in her clairvoyance, too many unknowns lurked beyond.

At that moment she would give anything to believe in crystal balls. But she would never forsake her fervent belief in the possibility of miracles existing. That faith was the most precious commodity in her arsenal of survival tools. It alone might be the most secret, most valuable and most necessary weapon of all the fittest in the human race.

Despite everything, she could not deny the desire she harbored for Knute Corsun. Desire growing inside her like a living embryo, bit by tiny bit, gaining strength as its own separate entity.

What ifs assailed her:

> *What if I went to him again, would he be responsive? What if he came here, would I receive him? What if I told him how I feel, what then? How would he react - surprised, bemused, indifferent? What if he felt the same, how would I act - mystified, relieved, afraid? What if I am not ready? What if I am? What if I never will be?*

If the barrage of questions swirling around in her head did not stop she just might go over the edge. If the battalion of voices whispering orders and advice were not stilled.....

Her inner demons were most taunting nights and during the days when she was alone. Solitude was the signal for them to come out in full swing. They cajoled and bantered like chattering banshees. And while they were frolicking in her mind, she was drawn and tense, waiting for the siege to subside. The more she stayed to herself, the more momentum they seemed to be gathering. She was learning that peace was possible but only at a very high premium. The stakes waged were costly, her privacy the sacrifice. Out of sheer desperation to rid herself of the inner clamor, she would comply. She had to learn to banish caution and, in the process conjure the nerve to set sail from familiar shores.

....

PART II

They were seated around the old oak table in Knute's makeshift dining room. He was telling Helmi about a place he had seen recently. The wonder in his voice was contagious and soon she was equally enthused.

Evidently, judging from his descriptions, it was an exquisite piece of property - a perfect realization of her decade-long quest in search of her ideal. If the farm existed, he had listened well to the frequent tangents she went off on, fantasizing about someplace she had never seen but knew she would someday. It did not matter that Knute, not she, finally discovered it. The important thing was that her patience and persistence, virtues she could gladly do without, were paying off at last.

Her fate suddenly hinged on a huge unknown - would the owners be willing to sell?

The mystery spot, so eerily like her vision, suddenly made her anxious about actually seeing it for the first time. Reality so rarely exceeded, or even came close to meeting her expectations.

She had an inkling, however, of something different this time. A turn, perchance, in the tides of her fortune. It was an exhilarating prospect, strange too, to feel such a strong surge of optimism, of elusive hope.....

It was not far from them, he said, maybe a couple of miles, or three, down the beach.

"I was delivering a machine part I'd traded to the adjacent farm. We got to talking and somehow it came up that the next door neighbor was thinking of putting her place on the market," the details slowly drifted out in response to Helmi's silent query.

"When we went over to take a look - no one was there, they use it mostly week-ends and summers" - he continued unprodded, "I couldn't figure how anybody could let it go. It's pure wild beauty, still left pretty much in its natural state, like a tiny slice of ancient rainforest. Acres and acres of wilderness in the heart of civilization."

His voice rose with his mounting interest. Helmi was beginning to catch the bug.

"Turns out the man who owned it killed himself sometime back - had some incurable disease and hung himself in the tool shed. Rumor is his survivors don't have the wherewithal for the upkeep. Also they were pretty hard hit by the circumstances of his sudden death," he filled in several gaps in the story.

"Metcalf, the neighbor, says the noose is still hanging in the shed just as Baylor left it when he went. Main trouble is he was fairly young judging by today's standards, only in his early sixties," he related, warming to the subject.

"Frankly I think they're too spooked by the whole thing to stay. Can't really blame' em but what a place to have to give up. Told Metcalf I knew of someone who might be interested in taking a look at it. Said he'd pass it on to the Baylors."

"I'm so very gratified you did. Thank you for doing that for me without my asking. It makes me think I might have a chance at it but I'll have to move quickly," Helmi said, extremely relieved. Hope was rising in her heart like a full moon slowly emerging from the forest.

"So far you've got as good a chance as any. No one else really knows about it 'cept for us, that it might come up for sale soon."

Helmi was thinking to herself that if it were at all true, it would be just about the luckiest thing that had ever happened to her.

She had not seen the property but was already giving thanks to her grandmother, so recently deceased, who was always quoting passages to her from the Bible like 'For everything there is a season'; 'If it's meant to be it will be'; 'When the time is ripe for it to happen, it will' - echoes of soothing words to steady her through the many months of negotiations that followed.....

An arch of mammoth pines, hemlocks and firs created shadowy dapples along the farm's approach road, anchored by feathery clumps of sword and bracken ferns. Long and rich in ancient mysteries it spoke to Helmi of other places, other times.

As they drove in she gasped. It looked uncannily like the country lane of her childhood, the one that took her to her grandparents' weathered log cabin in the woods. It had the same feel of peace, of stillness, a sense of long, lazy summer days. Lichen-draped branches, ivy-clad trunks, sunlight-speckled leaves; timeless, immortal, universal, exquisite.

Forever it seemed like she'd been searching for just such a spot. The rutty drive snaked its way through the grounds, surrounding a large oblong patch of grass. Huge flowering shrubs and trees dotted the pasture which served as front yard for the old shingled farmhouse. A woodshed stood to one side, stacked to the rafters with split firewood and kindling. A small clone of the main house at the end of the drive, faced with a cedar porch, was dwarfed by towering spruce and pines. In front one lone hemlock hovered over it like a sentinel. What looked like a little bunkhouse stood off to one side. Another barn-like structure sat wrapped in woods a bit further down the road.

She felt a stir of sadness for the general air of neglect and unkempt state of the place. But the chord of recognition it struck deep within her was so intense that she vowed, no matter what, to make it hers.

When the house was finally put up for sale, after a lot of vacillation, Helmi was one of the first to take the tour. She was careful not to look too closely at the house's rundown condition or the impossible layout, considering that it had only been a weekend or summer retreat. In that light it rose several rungs above the typical beach house.

People were sitting at a large table drinking coffee the day she went through. Friends of the Baylors down for the weekend, according to the realtor. The fire was she felt a warm rush as if the house were wrapping its arms around her in a welcoming embrace. From that moment on she
felt completely comfortable, at home as if she truly belonged there.

She knew in her heart it would be a huge strain on her finances for many years to come, would eat up everything she had earned and saved from the sale of her previous fixer but no amount of hardship would deter her. Not able to fathom living anywhere else she would find the formula for survival.

She was on her own - no Knute to hold her hand. She must

move fast, no hesitating, if she wanted to beat out the developers or wealthy tourists buying up property in the area. No time for reflection. This was one time her impetuosity would serve her well- a time she must act without hesitation or regret, must move forward boldly with direction and purpose.

Within hours, to her surprise, she was sitting in the realtor's office making an offer, not the exact asking price, but one that would be hefty enough to keep the owner's interest. She was shocked to learn that her timing was perfect. It had only been on the market a week, not enough time for any other offers. She could not believe her offer was accepted. With the earnest money being only minimal, she was well on her way to owning something envisioned most of her life, from those early days of her girlhood, wistful days spent gathering wildflowers around her grandparents' farm.

The only feasible way she could buy the place was to sign a contract for at least twenty years, possibly longer, with an interest rate well above the norm. The down payment also would have to be substantial. Not even these stringent demands would throw her off the scent. She was like a bloodhound sniffing its kill. She agreed to every new proposal presented her, until she thought she would crack under the strain, start screaming and never be able to stop. But by some minor miracle she weathered the grinding grist mill of negotiations until they came to a standstill and both sides were duly satisfied with the outcome.

Moving day, she well knew, was going to be the happiest day of her life. She could hardly wait but it would be another several months before all the loose ends were tied.

The remainder of her possessions were being kept in storage at the boarding house. They were minimal since she had gradually sold mostly everything before leaving the city, so as not to have as much to move.

Even then she sensed she would head west. Selling her things had been one way of making it closer to reality.....

....

Staring out to sea he watched the storm gather momentum and move rapidly shoreward. He was used to strong winds and high waves but not with near hurricane velocity like they predicted of this one. Small craft warnings were up. Hardly any vessels were out so he was shocked to see, looking down shore, where the rough swells had forced a crab boat to run aground. It had keeled over at an awkward tilt onto its side. The rudder and a good portion of its hull were deeply embedded in the sand. He didn't know how long it had been there but tractors and cranes were starting to arrive and far off he could hear a chopper coming. It was a strange and disturbing sight - the first time Knute had ever seen a forty foot trawler beached. He was totally baffled yet titillated by the intense drama and mystery of it.

A crowd was beginning to gather. Cars were streaming down the approach road, pulling up single file along the shore, as if parking to watch a drive-in movie.

The horizon was so fogbound that it was difficult to tell where sky met sea. The only visible things were the frothing white waves, foamy as a vast boiling cauldron.

Knute picked out what looked to him to be the co-skippers of the grounded vessel from the growing crowd milling around the vicinity. Patrol cars were strategically parked to ward off the curious from venturing too close to the rescue site. It was already crawling with huge cranes and plows scooping bucket upon bucket of sand out from under the boat and onto a pile that was rapidly swelling into a small mountain.

The two men appeared dazed, obviously bewildered by the nasty dilemma they had created. They steered clear of each other, aimlessly pacing back and forth, hands in pockets, heads lowered as they followed the salvage operation's progress.

One of the larger tugs from nearby Grayson Port was positioned offshore ready to pull. But first the chopper, trailing a huge length of steel cable, had to get near enough a ground worker so he could grab the end and hook it to the overturned boat. That done, it headed out to sea where it hovered for what seemed to be hours until, finally, it dropped the opposite end of the hauling line onto the tug and sped off, dwindling into the distance.

Then, inch by inch, the pulling phase began, as if trying to carefully yank out something stranded in quicksand - a delicate balance of forceful yet gentle persuasion.

It was sometime before Knute noticed any progress and then suddenly he thought he saw a slight shift in the boat's position. And then, yes! It had actually moved up a bit out of its shallow sandy grave. Again and again he watched the intricate ordeal. As the stark white Carla K struggled to right herself she looked almost like a wobbly foal trying to get to its feet during its first hour of life.

Several hours later the chaotic state of affairs, along with the storm, was subsiding. The crabber was slowly being dragged out to sea and down to the port for repairs. The cars and passersby were dispersing, the afternoon's excitement was winding down. People were heading home. The two captains drove off in the fire chief's truck. It was all over.

Knute felt slightly dazed himself. He'd never seen a fishing boat run amok before, nor any other floating vessel for that matter. It was unsettling to say the least. What could have caused the mishap? he wondered. Either something technical or else human error, he surmised. But which? He felt sorry for the two men and relieved that he hadn't been manning the craft himself. That was one debacle the likes of which he could honestly say he had never been guilty of causing. It was also a first for him to witness. It was the kind of day he would have trouble forgetting and, more than likely, his hyperactive memory would vividly recall it for many years to come. Too vividly.

He stayed on awhile even after most of the last stragglers had departed.

Soon he saw the fire chief's truck heading down the beach seemingly toward him but then realized it was the wreck spot he was targeting.

Curious as to what he was up to Knute stood watching nearby as the chief stepped down from the truck and started meticulously scouring the area.

But soon he was straying closer and closer to the scene until he was beginning to attract the chief's attention.

"Can I help you sir?" the chief barked gruffly. "This area is restricted."

"Don't mind me," Knute tossed back, between the din of wind and surf. "I was just trying to get a handle on what really went on here. Can't quite figure out how it could have happened."

As he spoke, Knute surveyed the hefty chief with the foghorn for a voice.

Fire Marshall Kendrick's big, burly body went with the size of his voice. He was stocky rather than obese and not as tall as he would like. He craved being noticed. And appreciated, and obeyed. But, above all, he demanded respect even when he couldn't command it.

He was known to family, friends and co-workers as Rusty. The nickname had stuck early on when it was clear his hair would always be the color of rust.

Not only did he like to boom out orders and instructions. He also thrived on throwing his weight around whenever the chance cropped up. Like it had that day. He was eking every last drop out of the latest of a steady stream of crises. His main order of business was to make sure everyone knew he, and only he, was in charge.

He was proud of his slow steady rise through the ranks of Parkhaven's Volunteer Fire Department of Klickimas County to chief. And he was very proud of how many cities and towns his duties, responsibilities and especially his authority encompassed.

Knute noticed a slight swagger to his stride and the huge, portable CB radio clipped to his wide black leather belt. From it raspy voices sporadically blurted out some source of trouble through the static. The chief didn't seem to hear.

He was sniffing the accident scene like a programmed bloodhound, methodically rather than rapidly. Periodically a tow truck driver, crane operator or policeman came to him and spoke briefly as he nodded and pointed. He pulled down the ribbon marker that had held the crowd at bay and threw it in the back of his truck. The red light was still flashing on top of the cab.

Knute inched a few feet nearer, this time within conversation range.

"Have they made a determination as to what caused her to go astray?" he queried cautiously.

Chief Kendrick didn't answer immediately. He acted preoccupied by some extremely important business that kept him from being bothered.

Finally he spoke, reluctantly, as if afraid of divulging some top secret information. Knute understood what they meant by the phrase "it was like pulling teeth".

"It looks, from the preliminary investigation, like the co-captain who was supposed to be manning the craft while the other one slept, accidentally took a little snooze himself, at the same time. The wind steered her for a long time until the only place left to go was ashore. They came all the way down the coast in the middle of the night without having had much sleep. Both of them just drifted off.....

"The one who messed up is down at the port on the telephone to the president of the company that owns the boat, resigning his position. Before they had a chance to fire him. He had the sense to know that anybody who did what he did doesn't deserve to be in the business. He found out the hard way that he's not cut out to be a skipper."

Knute was too stunned by the degree of negligence to speak.

By this time Chief Kendrick didn't need any prompting. He was extremely proud to be the sole source of such up-to-the-minute reportage of a major disaster in his territory.

"They're just lucky to have come out of it with their lives," Knute blurted, having
finally found his tongue. He was severely shaken. "It could have been fatal."

"And for their ship too," Chief Kendrick added. "But according to the crew checking her over she didn't sustain that much damage. Just some nicks and scratches and a few gouges. She'll be up and about in no time." He seemed almost sorry to have her leave the area.

....

Moving day finally arrived and Helmi was in the midst of a flurry of activity. Every so often she would stop what she was doing for a few minutes to savor the feeling of ecstasy flooding through her. As she predicted, it was something stronger than she had ever felt before.

Simultaneously she experienced a sense of calm in knowing that she had arrived at her final destination and pleasure at seeing all around her the culmination of an arduous journey. What gave her the greatest satisfaction was how closely everything resembled her initial vision from the beginning.

The royal purple moving van, parked in the entryway and seemingly as long as a block, was already there waiting for her.

She hurried Moongirl, her tranquilized cat, into the tiny annex down the road to ensure she would not try to escape from the unfamiliar territory. Helmi wondered how she would take to her new home once the drug's calming effect wore off.

Relieved to have Moongirl out of harm's way, she set about directing traffic in the main house, the workmen following her from room to room setting down the heavy furniture pieces. For only having seen the interior a couple of times, placement of each piece went surprisingly smoothly. Boxes of books were stacked in one of the lower floor rooms until she could arrange them in the upstairs library.

A real library at last, she thought to herself, and even more perfect, it had a fireplace. It would take a long time and a tremendous amount of hard work to make it look and feel like her own place but Helmi was not intimidated by the task at hand. She had already been through the same process twice before, with each of the projects double the size of the one before.

The remodeling of her last house had been challenging and

rewarding but nowhere near in scale to what she had just taken one.

As she was musing on this fact, she caught sight of a stranger approaching from across the road that ran alongside her property.

She immediately had mixed emotions. Some- one was coming onto her land uninvited and about to see her on her worst possible day, all sweaty and messy. And yet, how nice, she thought, it would be to have someone to welcome me and share in my excitement.

She was as tall as Helmi, and slender in a boyish, athletic way. Her heavily-peroxided hair was faded almost to white and severely wrapped into a tight knot at the nape of her neck. She walked proudly, striding boldly, squinting her small, high-set eyes in the sunlight while never taking them off Helmi's.

The movers were awaiting Helmi's instructions and she felt weak from fatigue.

"I just stopped over to welcome you to your new home. I'm Gwen Ashwood" she drawled. She had a slow, nasal type of voice.

"I'm Helmi Seaborne. Thanks for the hospitality," she mustered, momentarily revived.

"It's great to have you for a neighbor and to know you'll be next door," Gwen added.

"I've waited a long time for it. This is the happiest day of my life," Helmi confessed to this total stranger.

"I can see why," Gwen concurred, her eyes darting furtively in and out of various nooks and crannies around the property. "It's a special place."

And she turned on her heels and left as abruptly as she had arrived.

Helmi, relieved to get back to unloading her things, was mystified and more than a little intrigued.

She had an inkling that she might be looking at the back of one pretty odd duck.

She flashed back over the years she'd just spent remodeling her run-down house and garden in order to escape too-close or too-difficult neighbors. Privacy was, for her, such a precious commodity. And, here too, she meant to preserve and protect it at all costs. Already she could see it was not going to be easy.

The movers continued placing various large pieces of furniture throughout the rooms of the house, which was, for the most part in a sad state of repair.

But every time she glanced out one of the many windows and caught a glimpse of the land, or ran to the vast picture window and spotted the sea, her spirits lifted dramatically.

Shuffling everything throughout the house had thoroughly exhausted her. Leaving the movers in charge of bringing in the rest of the boxes and racks of clothes, she decided to explore the path that traversed her land and led down to the beach. The spreading ache in her limbs was so acute at that moment that it seemed to her even a brief glimpse of the sea and a short walk beside it would be the perfect panacea.

It was nearing the end of August, her favorite time of year. All the wild flowers were in their prime. A warm, fresh scent rose up as the wild strawberries were crushed beneath her sandals. Deep blue clumps of vinca and vetch bloomed profusely alongside patches of plum-colored beach peas. Around one corner of the trail, she spotted tall stalks of bright orange fireweed swaying gracefully with the wind. Her land formed a long, narrow rectangle with a vast forest of fledgling shore pines spreading clear down to the dunes.

But, to Helmi, the most exquisite sight of all was the lush green sea of wild grass abutting both sides of the path. It looked so inviting, as if beckoning her to lie down, stretch out against its silken slope of meadow and study the clouds. Another day she would, when she had more time. Right now all she wanted to do was reach the sea - to see it, smell and touch it, taste it.

She walked on for some time longer, absorbing everything, every insect, bee and butterfly. She especially loved the dragonflies and grasshoppers which always brought back happy memories from her youth. Buttercups, too, and ladybugs.

She could hear it, the steady drone like the distant sound of a busy freeway. She was so near - the noise was almost deafening. Then she mounted the last small incline, stood at its peak and sucked in her breath at the sudden spectacle. She felt as though the wind had nearly been knocked from her. She didn't know whether to laugh or cry or do both at once. And for a moment it seemed like she did a little of each. The overwhelming sensation flooding her was that she had found her way. She had come home.

Carrying her sandals in one hand she shuffled through the warm, dry sand, kicking it in the air a little as she went. Her feet tickled as it sifted through her toes.

She walked right down to the water's edge and waded in up to her ankles.

The ocean was warm and calm. A rich blue-black behind the frothy white sea foam of the waves.

Swarms of snowy plovers flitted first one way, then the other, white on one side, reversing to dark. Flocks of seagulls swooped, screeching out wild, spine-tingling calls.

No one else was on this stretch of beach except for a few children playing among the driftwood logs up near the dunes. Helmi reveled in the unfamiliar solitude. She could see it was a new-found nirvana that would be very difficult to leave. Not that she was planning to but even for a short trip sometime she would not want to go. A sense of peace surged through her, elevated her spirits, making her feel feather-like.

She walked for miles in one direction, then turned and walked for miles the opposite way. It was the perfect backdrop for "getting the cobwebs out of one's brain" as she referred to reflecting or meditating. It was also a sublime place to settle down, collect one's thoughts and daydream about the future.....

"I found your trail marker and thought I'd come check out how you're getting along in your new place," Knute Corsun said softly to Helmi's back.

She was kneeling in dirt, planting herbs in the kitchen garden near the front door. Knute's sudden appearance so startled her that she dropped her spade and swung around to meet his bemused gaze.

"Hope you don't mind my dropping by unannounced, but I was curious to find out what you think of this fancy spread. Is it suiting what it was you had in mind?"

"It couldn't be any more perfect if I'd designed it myself, thanks," she said smiling warmly. She was a little surprised at just how happy she was to see him. She felt a warm flush go all through her body as she looked into his tanned, weathered face. He wore a red checked logger's shirt and looked even better than he had the last time they met. He was an extremely welcome sight.

She stood up quickly and grabbed his hand before she had time to think about what she was doing. Knute smiled to himself. She was like a little girl excited to show off something new. It's a good sign, he thought. He especially liked spontaneous and enthusiastic people. He'd never known anyone more blessed with those qualities than Helmi. He found her more beguiling at that particular moment than at any other time since he had met her.

He was her willing captive as she gently pulled him along with her to inspect the grounds. There were so many favorite places to share with him, making it difficult to choose where to begin.

She led him down the road to a small cabin tucked into the trees. It looked like a miniature version of the main house with white clapboard siding and green shutters on either side of the small-paned windows.

A tiny porch covered by a corrugated fiberglass roof had several caved-in boards and a dry-rotted railing.

"The former owners rented this out to some man for the last three years," she explained as she opened the glass-paned front door. "He must have lived like an animal judging from the filthy condition he left it in. It's still disgusting but at least I've had a chance to air it out a bit. It's been fodder for the bugs so long there's hardly anything left."

"What are you going to do with it? It's pretty much a white elephant, isn't it? Knute asked skeptically. He could hardly breathe in the air, the mildew stench was so thick.

Helmi winced slightly. His careless remark wounded her pride somewhat more than she cared to admit. She loved the little house, in spite of its flaws, mostly because it belonged to her.

"I want to fix it up into a guest house, a place where my friends and family can come and stay," she retorted a trifle too defensively. He hadn't meant to hurt her feelings, she knew.

She always got a little snappish when she was tired. She was still too excited, her surroundings too new for her to sleep very well.

"I think it's worth saving if only for the beautiful floors under this moldy carpet. The old windows alone would cost a fortune to replace."

"Depends on what condition the foundation and exterior walls are in. Might be cheaper to start from scratch," he persisted.

"I think I'll have a construction company take a look at it and give me an estimate as to how much it might be to repair," she said stubbornly. She didn't give up easily on something she believed in, like this potentially charming cottage. She already had a fixed vision of how it could be with some tender loving care.

"Maybe I could help you with it," Knute surprised her by saying quietly. "I've done some remodeling projects in my time. I could get you some bids on lumber costs, etcetera."

"That would be lovely," Helmi nodded. "One thing I do know is it's too much for me to handle by myself. Let's go look at the carport. I want to tell you my idea for it."

It, too, sat snugly in the midst of a copse of trees, just down the road from the cabin. Built of peeled lodge-poles, it was rustic, open on the sides and covered with a thick cedar shake roof. Two cars could be housed side by side inside it to partially protect them from the harsh coastal elements. It stood empty and desolate looking now.

"I found out from my neighbor, Mr. Metcalf, that it was built over ten years ago by Mr. Baylor, the previous owner, completely out of driftwood that he'd gathered himself down on the beach. Even the shakes for the roof he split himself from driftwood.

"What are you planning to use it for?" Knute asked, genuinely curious.

"Well," Helmi began, "I've had a lot of time to decide what I want to do with this place, while the paperwork for the sale was being drawn up. I've always wanted to own my own horse ever since I was a little girl but my family wasn't too keen on the idea. I've been dreaming for quite a long time about a small ranch with a barn and pastures for my horse. Maybe even breed it someday. And down the trail behind the house there would be great running space on the beach, in fact thirty miles of track. It's something I've always envisioned, riding horseback beside the ocean. I have the property. There's enough land for an upper and lower pasture if fencing were built. And this shed would make a perfect two-stall barn with a paddock area in front if the sides and back were enclosed. That tiny bunkhouse could be the tack room. Now all I need is the horse. I've even got an idea about where to get that."

"Let me guess," Knute needled her playfully. "A Kentucky Thoroughbred farm."

Helmi laughed, "How well you know me. But seriously I don't think I'd know what to do with a Thoroughbred. It would definitely be too much horse for my skills. Actually I was thinking of a very gentle-spirited horse I've known for quite some time." She slowly drew in her breath, letting the suspense gather momentum. She watched Knute's eyes light up with curiosity. He was definitely intrigued.

"And do I also know this horse?" he inquired.

"As a matter of fact you do," she was preening like a peacock, proud of the secret she'd kept to herself for so long and was about to reveal.

"And does this horse have a name?" he lightly prodded her to tell him more.

"As a matter of fact it does," she smiled.

"And might I be so lucky as to know the name of this mystery horse with the gentle spirit?"

"It wouldn't mean anything to you. It's a name I came up with myself after I got to know her somewhat. I call her Windflower, after the sea anemone that grows wild in this region. She's boarded on the land you manage for the Bureau." She could see the surprise register on his face. He wasn't expecting her answer to have anything to do with his horses.

"You mean Lily, our five-year-old Appaloosa mare," he said. "We named her that because she's speckled like the Oriental lily. I like your name better. It suits her. She's high-spirited and, if given half the chance, can run like the wind. She's very elemental. Loves to run free in the fresh air, is drawn to fire, likes to roll in the earth and the beach is one of her favorite places to go."

"There's something very special about her," Helmi said almost reverently. "I felt a rapport with her the first time we met. It was a rare feeling, something I've hardly ever experienced before. We formed a potent kinship with each other from that very first moment. For me it happens more often with horses than it does with people."

"For me, too," Knute said as his eyes told her of his mounting regard. He was glowing with pleasure, pleased with her appreciation and affection for his horse, for sharing her secret with him, for being the way she was.

She was profoundly moved by the eloquence of his eyes. They held her captive with their intense, steady gaze, not wavering for an instant.

She drew in her breath as if gathering strength to continue.

"I was wondering," she proceeded cautiously, "if there would be any chance of adopting Windflower, I mean Lily, from the BLM. I would provide a good home for her and take extra good care of her. She would be like my own child at least in the beginning. After she learns to trust me we'll be a team."

"I hadn't expected anything like this," he said frankly. "But now that you brought it up, I can't think of any reason not to. In fact it's starting to make a lot of sense. You two, knowing you both as I do, would be perfect for each other. A match made in heaven. In fact, I'm just sorry I hadn't thought of it myself."

Helmi gave a slight sigh of relief, "I was hoping you would see it that way. I really do want her and she seems to have some feeling for me."

"I'll see what I can do to insure that it happens the way you've pictured it," Knute promised. "It should work out OK. There would probably be some sort of nominal fee, mostly a formality, the standard minimum. I'm sure they'd be glad to have one less mouth to feed. Another thing is they're in charge of so many throughout the Western states that one less will hardly be missed. I'll check into it and let you know."

"If they agree to it, I'll have to get the pastures fenced in and the carport converted into the barn right away. Then we can transfer Windflower over here soon after that. I can hardly wait," Helmi said, her voice rising as she thought how it might be possible to happen the way she'd always dreamt it would.

"Just thought I'd mention I've built miles of fences and helped put up my share of barns if you need me for getting the place ready for Lily," Knute offered.

"You make it sound as though it's a pretty sure thing," Helmi said.

"Practically a done deal," Knute said reassuringly as if trying to calm her sudden case of nerves.

"I hope you're right. I don't know what I'd do without her

now that I've grown so attached to her. Not that anyone could really possess her, she's too much of a free spirit for that. But at least I could keep her in relative comfort and provide her with loving companionship just as she could bring endless hours of enjoyment to me. All my life I've wanted a horse of my own but it didn't seem meant to be until now."

"There's a good possibility it could become a reality," Knute said with genuine conviction. It would mean less for him to look after.

"Well if we can pull it off then I certainly could use your help and would be grateful for it. Thanks for the offer," Helmi said with relief.

"I can see how simple it would be to convert this carport into a two-stall barn in no time. Basically close in the back and sides, put up rails around the front paddock area, install gates, extend the loft floor for more ceiling and that's all there is to it," Knute explained.

"I love its lodge-pole style," Helmi enthused. "It looks so rustic and rugged. Perfectly suited for a ranch and it should be perfect for Windflower too."

"You've got a great spot here," Knute agreed. "Everything you need, all the ingredients to keep a horse fat and sassy. There's enough land for at least two pastures, maybe add more later, cut back toward the ocean. We should get the barn done before we tackle the fences. Provide a roof over her head before the rains come."

All the while he spoke, gesturing to make certain points, Helmi studied him, liking more of what she saw by the minute. Something about him intrigued her in a mystifying way. He was different from anyone she'd ever known, but she couldn't put her finger on just what it was.

As they continued on their tour, Helmi gently prodded him to reveal more of himself. He seemed pleased that she showed an interest in his origins and obliged her with his reply, as if it were an opportunity to relieve himself of a heavy burden.

"I was born and raised in central Oregon. My mother died before I was ten, from complications giving birth to my baby brother. My father was gone a lot, traveling to his different logging sites, so we - there were eight of us - were mostly brought up by our aunt, one of his sisters. She was widowed and had lost her own child so she came to live with us. The old man was drunk most of the time when he was off the job and even at work too, later on. Finally he hardly came around to see us at all. I can barely remember him, but what I do recall aren't very pleasant memories. He missed my mother something awful. Never got over her death. She was so young. I can barely remember anything about her either except that everybody said she was indescribably beautiful.

"Aunt Callie tried to fill us in on our family roots but it was all pretty sketchy," Knute went on. "Just vague snatches of mostly hearsay, basically their people's oral history handed down through the generations.

"I remember Dad raging about how all the land was stolen away from his people. He claimed that his grandfather was one of the joint ruling chiefs of the Nez Perce Indians living on a reservation in Northern Idaho. He was always very proud of his Native American blood, but also very angry about how wronged they were by the government agencies constantly taking away vast tracts of land he claimed had been owned by them. Everywhere we went, he would point and say, 'This used to belong to us before they robbed us blind'.

"We were dirt poor," he continued, uncoaxed, "but always managed to have at least one horse, sometimes more. I practically learned how to ride before I could walk. By the time I'd taken the land management job I'd already worked with at least fifty horses. They're as much a part of me as breathing. I can tell you one thing. You'll have one hell of a good horse if you end up with Lily, or Windflower, as you call her. She's smart, tough and loyal. Good instincts, too."

"She seems almost human," Helmi added to his list of accolades. "It's as if she understands everything I tell her."

"She probably does. She's used to me talking to her ever since she was just a tiny foal, one of the smallest I've ever seen." He was going to miss her, he could feel it in his gut. But she was going to a good home, to someone who would love her no matter what and where he would still be able to see her often.

They had come to the woods that were bisected down the middle by the approach road. It was one of Helmi's favorite places, one of the main reasons she had bought the property. Again she flashed back to her grandparents' farm where she had spent weekends and vacations, driving through the forest and down the long, steep, rutty road to get there. Two places so alike it was almost eerie, only hers had the ocean too.

Someday, Helmi mused to herself, I'd like to carve out some riding trails in the forest lining either side of the drive. It wouldn't be much, just enough for a little change of scenery. She had always loved to ride through the woods. It was so relaxing and scenic, too.

They walked over the grounds mapping out how to prepare the two pastures - one upper and one lower.

....

PART III

It was an early evening in May. A spectacular sunset had just put on its nightly display with an especially flamboyant flourish. No matter what the weather did during the rest of the day, by sundown, its sky palette was always cleared of any cloudy interference, calmly awaiting the sun's sweeping brushstrokes.

Knute had made the familiar trek to Helmi's along the beach after finishing up his own chores. It was his first day on the job. He had already ordered the lumber he would need and had brought his carpentry tools over earlier.

Helmi was there to greet him with a wide, welcoming grin. She felt incredibly fortunate that he was so skillful a builder and that he had offered to help with the barn and pastures. A sudden wave of gratitude washed over her when she saw him coming up the trail from the beach.

"Would you like some dinner before you get started?" she asked, hoping he'd be hungry enough to join her.

"Thanks but I've already eaten, such as it was. Filling anyway - eat mostly just to keep up the energy."

"Sounds like you think you're not much of a cook," Helmi said teasingly.

"I can take or leave any food I fix, doesn't much matter. Tastes all the same to me anyway. Main thing is sustenance," he confessed somewhat sheepishly.

"Everything you've cooked for me has been OK. Simple, honest fare done to perfection."

"Glad to hear it, but it's not really my bag," he insisted.

"Well maybe you can join me for coffee after I've eaten. You might be ready for a short break by the time I've cleaned up the dishes.

He sensed she seemed a trifle forlorn about something. He wished he could cheer her up somehow. If he worked extra hard to do a good job, he thought, maybe then. He felt an overwhelmingly strong desire to please her, to gain her trust and confidence. She seemed to him, at that moment like some sort of wild bird which, if provoked might suddenly take flight never to return.

"Sounds tempting," he said to her over his shoulder as he headed out to get started. "I'll see you after awhile."

She set about getting her dinner ready while sipping a glass of chilled white wine and watching the news on the tiny TV sitting on the counter.

She thought, *How lonely a business it is to fix and eat my meals alone everyday and every evening except on the rare occasions I go out. I don't think I'll ever get used to being alone. I just wasn't cut out of the cloth to be an old maid and will never reconcile myself to a doddering spinster-hood. My marriage was so short-lived and sorry an excuse for one that it's hard to believe I ever was wed. It was such a long time ago that it's sometimes hard not to still think of myself as a fair and pure young thing. Or maybe the stare Knute sometimes sears me with suddenly makes me feel so vulnerable. His hazel eyes, peering aloofly out from beneath those long, black lashes hold more soulful mystery than any I've ever seen. They are a most compelling reason why I'd like to try and get to know him better.*

After she'd finished up the dinner dishes she brewed some fresh-roasted Italian coffee and carried a big mug full out to Knute. He was deeply immersed in his task of hammering up the stack of eight-foot-long standard boards to the back corner posts of the barn.

He looked up and saw her coming and doffed his hat with a smile, "How'do, ma'am. Smells like mighty good coffee you've got there." He quickly reached to take it from her, to help ease her burden She kept her own cup and leaned back against one of the posts to take a sip.

"How's it coming?" she asked somewhat apprehensively, not knowing quite what to expect but trusting him instinctively to do a good job.

"So far, so good," he managed to say in between sips. He'd never tasted coffee as good as that before. "I got the best quality wood they had available. Extra thick standard board, hardly any knots. I'm starting to close in the back south wall first to keep as much of the elements out as possible, then I'll do the side rails. It shouldn't take more than a couple of days to finish this part. I'll have to build four gates - two for the stalls and the other two for the entrances to the paddock area but first posts have to be set to attach them to. Then there's the hardware to fit and plywood and beams to extend the ceiling out over the paddock area. After I get all that finished I'll start on the fencing around the lower pasture."

I like the way it's starting to look already," she said approvingly. "I can visualize exactly how it's going to look and with the driftwood lodge-poles and shake roof it will be just right."

"By the end of this week I'll have the fence boards and treated supports delivered. We'll need around thirty posts not counting the gate and they'll have to be sunk at least three feet deep," he told her.

"I want it to look more like garden fencing than pasture fencing so let's put the boards on the outside of the posts. A little unconventional but it will look a lot better, at least to me," Helmi bade him emphatically.

"The other way would lend more support as far as keeping the animal in the pasture, especially if she were to lean or push against one of the rails," Knute cautioned. "But it's up to you, whichever you prefer."

"I've never been known for my practicality. I'll take my chances and go with the outside."

About a month had passed since they first applied to the BLM requesting the adoption of Windflower by Helmi. Within two weeks, Helmi had her written consent and finalization papers to sign. She could "take possession" as soon as her property was out-fitted with the necessary facilities. Helmi had imagined the exact scenario for so long that the conversion layout for her would-be ranch was clear in her mind by the time her petition was accepted. During the third week Knute had begun taking measurements and ordering needed supplies and materials.

Meanwhile Helmi's excitement was mounting, knowing at the end of it all Windflower would be coming to live with her on the ranch permanently. Her first horse, her very own ranch. She began wondering what to name the ranch. It would have to have just the right nuance, a certain panache, and be a fitting tribute to the lyricism, to the poetry of the land.....

After considering several dozen different names for the ranch, she finally latched onto the word Wildwood and tried it out loud to see how it would sound: *Wildwood.* She let the word roll over her tongue gently. *It has a certain ring.....Wildwood Ranch.....a certain mystical, almost spiritual aura that reminds me of the mountain resort I stayed at so long ago with the same name.....a blissfully peaceful retreat surrounded by tall timbers, nature trails and the freshest air, just like it is here.....*

At last she felt she had a name that suited her secret haven, reflecting its enigmatic essence.

Knute agreed that it was perfect when she told him. "It has a noble sound about it," he had said. Also he could visualize how well it would look across the wood sign that would someday top the entrance posts, something else he offered to make. He seemed to be getting more deeply enmeshed in the place every day which filled Helmi with relief. Her attachment to him was running stride for stride with his for the ranch like a horse race. And, too, every so often there were subtle signs of his feeling for her............

A pickup loaded down with a half ton of grass hay was coming down the drive. Knute was waiting near the barn, ready to buck the bales up into the loft. He motioned the driver to back up closer to the ladder, then together they hoisted the bales overhead.

It was a warm, sunny day early in June, almost a year since Helmi had moved in. She stood on the front porch watching the two men, as the sweet aroma of the freshly-cut hay floated toward her. She felt a keen sense of satisfaction as she surveyed the scene. The upper and lower pastures were finished, fenced, with thickets of lush green grass dotted with pink and white clover blossoms. Each one included over an acre of land.

The carport was now a full two-stall barn with lodge-pole supports and a rustic roof of thick cedar shakes. A small paddock adjoined the front section.

Everything was in readiness for Windflower's arrival.

Knute was spending more and more time with Helmi at the ranch. He showed up early most mornings, after his own chores were done and the horses turned out for the day. He headed straight for the house, eager for a cup of Helmi's French-roasted coffee. They usually sat at her dining room table and, sipping slowly, went over the schedule for the day. From the dining room window they could see all of the lower pasture, the barn, guesthouse and grounds around the house.

The morning was so warm and sunny that they decided to move out to the old picnic table on the grass beside an ancient rhododendron. According to her neighbor, Mr. Metcalf, the previous owner, Baylor, had hand-hewn it himself out of driftwood he'd gathered on the beach. The benches too. It was one of the things on the property Helmi had instantly fallen in love with.

"When do you think we should plan on moving Windflower over here?" Helmi was asking expectantly. She could hardly contain her excitement at the thought of actually having Windflower with her every day.

"I'd say we're ready anytime now," Knute replied, just as anxious to see Windflower in such an exquisite setting. He couldn't help being pleased with the extensive work he'd done and more than a little curious as to how the mare would react to her new home. He smiled to himself at the thought of just how jubilant she would be, knowing her lively spirit.

"Well today is Wednesday. What about this Saturday? We could caravan her down the beach from the BLM property to here. It probably isn't much more than two miles away, wouldn't you say?" Helmi wondered.

"I'd guess closer to three," Knute replied. "But it's still within easy walking distance. She's an Appaloosa. They're a rugged breed and besides horses are capable of going much further than that in a day. Saturday should be fine."

"I'll have everything ready at this end," Helmi said. "But what about tack equipment and other supplies. What all will she need?"

"She'll have all of her gear with her when she gets here. We can carry most of it in backpacks and whatever won't fit in, I can bring over in the truck later. There isn't that much."

He had finished his second cup of coffee and was restless to get to work. He had a few loose ends to tie up in the upper pasture and the trail to clear leading down to the beach. The residue of several severe windstorms in a row, fallen pines and large branches lay strewn across the very pathway they would be bringing Windflower along.

And besides, he thought, *I can't keep sitting so near her, smelling her perfume, breathing in the fragrance of her skin, without touching her, holding her, wanting her.*

He excused himself abruptly and hurried off in the direction of the tool shed.

How mysterious he is, Helmi mused. She could never quite guess what he was thinking or had on his mind. He spoke so seldom and hardly ever about anything having to do with himself.

On Saturday, Windflower's arrival day, Helmi was up at dawn. Coffee mug in hand, she stood at the kitchen window studying the pinkish glow spreading in the east beyond the pines that surrounded the barn. Too soon to see much, though not too early to tell it would be a stunning sunrise and glorious, sunny day.

Everything was ready - the fresh bucket of water, sacks of feed, the tiny tack room swept and tidy and a loft full of sweet-smelling, just-harvested grass hay.

She and Knute had arranged to meet on the BLM property

around 11:00. "I'll be over after I've finished my breakfast and morning chores," she'd told him.

With so much to occupy her the morning sped by until, around quarter to 11:00, she started up her 4-wheeler and headed off toward Knute's.

He was waiting for her by the pasture gate, having fed and watered the horses and checked up on them before they set out.

They walked together toward the barn where Windflower was stabled.

"She senses something different in the air. Been pacing back and forth in her stall all morning, snorting and pawing and carrying on as if begging to be let in on the secret," Knute told her.

"I'm not surprised," Helmi said. "All her senses are so acute that she seems to respond almost telepathically sometimes to things."

"It's a well known fact that many horses have highly developed extra sensory perception besides their powers of mental telepathy. She's probably one of the best mind readers you'll ever run across," Knute explained.

"I've already experienced her impressive skill at empathizing with certain other horses and also at anticipating my moods and actions. She's sharp to say the least. It's like a special gift she has but evidently it's not unique just to her," Helmi, fascinated, prodded him to go on.

"No. Like I said, most horses have it, but some to a much greater degree," he continued patiently. It was a vaguely gray area in the equine world, but one he fully embraced as being important to study and comprehend. Its potential as having positive ramifications with regard to humans communicating with horses was enormous.

Someday he hoped to do more research into the subject. Maybe even record his findings in a book. But that was probably a long way off, he supposed.

Helmi was ecstatic to see Windflower again. She felt like she'd been injected with a potent mood elevator every time she saw her. And the same seemed to be true for Windflower as well. She was dancing around her stall, whinnying a red-carpet welcome to Helmi, never taking her eyes off her slightest gesture. Not only did she remember her, but seemed to have been watching vigilantly for her to return.

They sniffed each other, nose to nose. Windflower nodded her approval at the familiar scent. The age-old greeting seemed to settle her as if she instinctively knew she could trust the woman who had gradually become such a loving friend.

"She seems to know you all right and really care about you," Knute observed, extremely impressed by the way they had bonded so totally in such a short time. "She doesn't take to too many, not even any of the other horses as a rule."

"I feel so close to her that at times it seems as if I had her out of my own body," Helmi confessed her deep maternal instincts.

"You even look quite a bit alike," Knute teased. "Same facial features, long legs and bone structure."

"I'm not exactly sure how I should take that," she laughed, "but now that I think about it, I accept it as a very great compliment."

"It was meant to be," he agreed, looking down at the ground, suddenly shy. He wasn't accustomed to praising women. "You're both very exquisite looking creatures."

"Thank you" was all she could muster a little breathlessly. Somewhat shaken by his obvious admiration, she was also secretly pleased and excited. He had never been quite so blatant about his feelings for her.

Knute shifted uncomfortably, juggling the unaccustomed weight of his emotions with an all too familiar state of arousal.

They were in the center aisle of the barn leaning against the wall of Windflower's stall.

"We'd better get moving if we're going to get her to your place and settled in by sundown," he suggested. "We still have to have a bite to eat before we start off."

They walked back to the cabin where he fixed a hearty midday meal of vegetable soup with chunks of beef along with huge egg salad sandwiches. Helmi could hardly move after they'd finished eating and wanted to do nothing more than stretch out for a long, lazy afternoon siesta.

She felt somewhat revived from the second wind she got sipping Knute's home-made rich, brown ale out of a large tumbler. It was difficult to leave until suddenly it dawned on her that the long awaited moment of Windflower's arrival was close at hand.

She leapt to her feet feeling the rush of adrenalin, causing Knute to grin widely.

"You're like a skittish young colt," he warned her. "You'll have to calm way down if we're going to keep Windflower in hand and away from charging or bolting."

"Do you really think she would? She's always behaved so well whenever we've been together."

"There's always the possibility if something out of the ordinary provokes her. That includes unusual noises or any kind of strange fracas."

"I'll be on my best behavior," Helmi promised like a rebuked child. "One thing I don't want to spawn is a nervous horse, though I'll admit patience and repose aren't two of my strongest suits."

"You're doing fine just as you are. You just have to remind yourself sometimes that horses are like young children who need love, security and especially discipline."

They were in the tack room inside the barn where Knute selected a leather halter and lead rope from the many hanging in a row along the wall.

When they reached Windflower's stall she nickered a soft welcome to them and impatiently pawed the dirt floor with her front hoof.

"She's already guessed that today's the big day and is anxious to get on with it," he said as he sniffed familiarly into the mare's nostrils a fond farewell greeting.

As Helmi opened the stall door he led the high-spirited filly out into the center aisle, then through the large sliding double wood exit doors and outside. She was prancing her own little jig of excitement, hardly able to keep her pent-up energy under control.

Knute spoke softly to her, his voice hardly above a whisper. She responded to its singsong rhythm by quickly quieting down, ready to tackle the task at hand. She was used to keeping the rare sense of aliveness she possessed under wraps when her handler was around. That, she knew, was when he wanted her to pay attention, be all business,
no acting up. Pleasing him meant a handful of molasses-tasting treats or a big, red, juicy Delicious apple, a particular favorite of

hers.

"She seems eager to please you," Helmi marveled at the two of them walking harmoniously in sync. "You have a special way with her, I see."

"It comes from years of experience, of listening, observing, learning to understand and communicate with them."

"But I think yours is more an innate touch, an instinctive sense of each horse being a unique individual," she told him. "It's a rare gift to have. You're one of the truly blessed."

"I think you have the same inner voice telling you how to deal with each situation as it arises. All you need now is more experience and more practice. It just takes time."

They were nearing the end of the long, grassy trail to the beach where they would then head north to her ranch.

Windflower was keenly alert, ears flicking back and forth, listening to the surf and all the seaside sounds. She seemed completely content and comforted by the familiar voices talking animatedly beside her. Her curiosity and boundless enthusiasm for so many new sights amused Knute and Helmi, filling them with delight.

She was used to exercising with Knute beside the sea but had never been very far from home. Today would be the longest distance she had ever traveled and she was filled with anticipation and expectation as to what she might find at the end of the journey.

There was no need to hurry. It was a long walk to Helmi's trail and they didn't want to risk tiring Windflower. She seemed perfectly happy to walk steadily beside them, although once in awhile her spirit got the better of her and she would prance in a wide circle around Knute.

Tossing her head and tail, trying to draw his attention away from Helmi, it was as if she were trying to say, "Look at me. I'm the prettiest, the smartest, the cleverest, not she."

"She's a handful, that's for sure," Knute smiled, "but she never gets too far out of control. Basically she's an easy keeper as they say."

"It will be fun learning her special ways, her different moods, calls and signals, that most horses have," Helmi told him. "They will be much easier to study and translate now that I'll be working with her on a daily basis."

"She's quite a character," he added. "She loves to play tag and hide and seek and race anybody that's handy from the pasture to the gate. She'll put on a highly entertaining show for anyone she suspects of being the slightest bit timid by rearing up on her hind legs and pawing the air with her front hooves. It's quite a spectacle to behold and not amusing for the faint-hearted. It's mostly all bluff, just a game she's playing, only the greenhorns don't know it."

"She's definitely a tease, I can see that," Helmi admitted. "And sassy, too, the way she swings her head around from side to side. I'd even go so far as to say she's got a little bit of an attitude problem. Is that part of your training regimen?" she asked teasingly.

"That comes to her naturally," he assured her, mimicking her mocking tone, "same as she was born wild. It's in her blood, to run free, even if it's only fantasy, since she'll always be a captive of sorts."

"I'll always provide her with as much space and freedom as I can possibly manage," Helmi vowed in a much more serious vein.

They had traveled about a mile and a half down the beach with Windflower showing not the least sign of tiring.

Her breed was known for its endurance on long treks and in grueling circumstances as in the days when they were the rugged steeds of the Nez Perce Indians.

That was one of the main reasons Helmi had been attracted to the horse in the first place, being, as she was, so passionate about anything to do with Native Americans.

It was nearly another mile and a half before they would arrive at Helmi's. The sun was high in the sky and beating relentlessly down on them.

"Wouldn't you know we'd pick one of the hottest days of the year to make this little sojourn," Knute remarked dryly.

"I don't mind it a bit. It feels great," Helmi said, lazily arching her neck back to let her face bask in the heat. "It's so rarely decent weather around here, I rather relish it."

"You're right about that," he concurred. "We're more used to hurricane-velocity winds and driving rainstorms. A good sight more days are filled with thunder and lightning than they are with sunshine. Last year alone we had over a hundred inches of rainfall. Might as well be living in a goddamn rainforest."

Helmi laughed, "You're just like everybody else I've met around here - always complaining about the weather. It's the biggest scapegoat of them all - always taking the rap for every other thing that's wrong with the world."

"Too true, too true," he nodded. "We've got to have something to blame our blasted troubles on . And it can be plenty of trouble when a forty foot Hemlock uproots and comes crashing down in front of you or a giant spruce snaps a few trusses in the roof of your house as it keels over."

"Sorry. It sounds like you've had firsthand experience with nasty windstorms," she empathized.

"And with mudslides and floods and droughts and, and, and," he added somewhat bitterly. "You name it, I've been through it and lived to tell about it."

"Well at least you haven't had to brave a Tsunami or a volcanic eruption."

"Only medium-sized quakes and the volcano blew too far away to affect me personally, but the Tsunami could be coming any day now. They're predicting one of the biggest earthquakes of all time could be hitting sometime soon," he said somewhat volatile himself.

"And you believe them?" she asked incredulously.

"You bet I do. These are seismologists and geological experts who have been studying fault lines and susceptible topography for decades. They're fully convinced of the possibility. People around here are starting to wake up and prepare for a natural disaster in the event of it occurring."

Suddenly they spotted the bright orange and white buoy tied to a driftwood post that marked the start of Helmi's trail. With mutual sighs of relief they veered Windflower away from the beach, pointing her nose in the direction of her new home.

She was immediately aware of the changing terrain. They stepped gingerly through dry sand as they made their way to the huge mounds of sea grass-covered dunes.

It was all great sport for Windflower who quickly lowered her head and snipped off a mouthful of the tall, willowy reeds.

Knute just as quickly reached down and tugged a handful out

of her jaws. "Oh no you don't," he cautioned her in a warning tone. "That's razor grass for the good reason that it could easily slit your tongue and lips. Come on girl, give it over. Besides you're not allowed to eat on the trail. You'll have the bridle on and hardware in your mouth, making grazing a bit trickier."

Snorting loudly, she stomped her disapproval at having such a tasty morsel yanked out of her grasp and pinned her ears back in protest.

They couldn't help laughing at her display of outrage.

"Oh don't be so touchy," Knute told her, giving her ear a playful tweak.

"You're going to have to learn that you can't get your way very often, if ever. Helmi's your new boss. She's in charge, not you. You'll always have to remember that."

She gave him a scornful look as if to say, "We shall see about that", shook her head and stepped onto the trail.

Right away she sensed it was different than the trail she was used to. Her whole body seemed to gear up for the new adventure. All her senses were aroused and her movements quickened. As she looked from side to side at the vast field of grass as far as the eye could see, her wonder gathered momentum until she was literally dancing up the path.

Knute, watching her intently, said "I've never seen her quite like this. She loves it! Look at her eyes. They're alive with excitement and I could swear she's smiling."

Moving through a large copse of shore pines, they rounded a bend. Down a short incline, in a clearing before them, lay the newly created pastures awaiting Windflower's arrival.

Knute opened the gate to the lower section, led Windflower in, released her from the lead rope and turned her loose.

Exploding like some jet-propelled rocket, around and around she ran through the lush green field of tall grass at a dizzying pace, leaping in a row of little bucks, rearing up and charging as she came down.

Having spent her store of excess energy, she was calm enough to begin grazing. She chomped with the zeal of an infant suckling its mother.

"I'd say she's quite passionate about her new home," Helmi laughed.

"I'd say that's the understatement of the century," Knute said, thoroughly delighted with the mare's reaction to her new surrounding.

Leaning against the fence together they relished watching her gorge herself and enjoy exploring the unfamiliar territory.

"I never dreamed it would be such a successful transfer. She acts as if she's completely content here," Helmi said in amazement.

"It doesn't take long for a horse to adjust if it's comfortable in its environment," Knute explained. "They're creatures of habit and routine and like to feel safe and secure. You've provided the type of setting any horse would love."

"I hope so," she sighed. "Lord only knows how hard I've tried to make a good home for her."

"She's in paradise," Knute assured her. "She's frolicking around like a kid in a candy shop. Look at the way she keeps running over to sniff you. She's attempting to bond with you which is the ultimate sign of trust and affection."

"I can't believe how much I already love her and want us to be friends," Helmi admitted.

"She senses that instinctively. You two are a good match for each other and I predict you will develop an unusually deep relationship - unique and rare between a human and a horse," he told her.

"There's something very special about her, some aura so elusive that I can't seem to put my finger on it," she said.

"I know what you mean," he said sympathetically. "I've felt the same way ever since I first laid eyes on her. It's like she possesses some potent magical spirit that the ancient gods endowed her with."

"That's it exactly," Helmi concurred. "How 'bout a cold beer," she offered. " I bet you've got a powerful thirst after such a long walk. We deserve a reward."

"Don't mind if I do. Thanks," he answered with a smile of relief.

She handed him a can of ice-cold brew. She didn't care for beer but joined him by sipping a glass of chilled white wine.

"I can't thank you enough for helping me to get her here," she said with genuine gratitude. "I couldn't have done it without you."

"My pleasure," he was drawn to her like a magnet by the warm tone of her voice. "She doesn't present much of a challenge in the way of causing problems. She just needs more handling. With practice and experience you'll have yourself one hell of a riding horse."

"How long does it usually take to train a horse?" she asked, intrigued.

"It all depends on the individual horse and a variety of factors concerning each one. For instance its temperament, how much handling it's had before starting it and innate intelligence. Physical condition, natural ability and attitude also figure into how it will progress."

"It seems to me you mentioned very early on that she'd had a traumatic accident when she was just a foal," Helmi said.

"That's right. Hardly more than a weanling. Barely six months old when a cub bear got into the pasture somehow and chased her over a fence that she was too small to clear. Her back legs must have got caught on the top slat. Somehow she managed to yank herself free and landed on the other side of the fence but was pretty badly hurt. I found her barely conscious. I covered her with a heavy blanket and put a thick matting of bedding straw under her. Luckily I had some Butte tablets to give her for the pain and a supply of penicillin to inject her with to fight off infection." He took a deep breath and continued.

"It turned out she had wrenched her left rear hip joint completely out of its socket. I had to dope her up heavily and pop it back into place myself. She had to stay off it for several days, but was so sore she didn't seem to mind too much. After the initial shock and ache were gone, I got her on her feet and walking around at least a half hour twice a day to keep the stiffness from setting in. She's a real little fighter and came around in no time but she's still got the tell-tale remains of a limp. She's strong-boned though and with the proper nutrition and exercise therapy she should come all the way back to being one hundred percent sound again."

Helmi had been listening raptly. He'd never talked much about the accident before.

"I thought I noticed a hint of her favoring one of her hind

legs," she said. "Now I understand why. It's amazing how barely noticeable it is after such a serious injury."

"Once she's gentled it would be a good idea to start her on a strict conditioning regimen to keep her back end limber and moving correctly," he advised her.

"What exactly would this so-called conditioning program consist of?" she asked, in a voice full of curiosity.

"First of all, to ready her for the saddle and rider, I recommend a rigorous ground-training exercise routine." He was trying to prepare her as gradually as he could for the long road ahead for Windflower's full recovery.

"Such as?" she prodded him to go on.

"Such as getting her used to the lunge line," he explained. "You've got the perfect outdoor arena to lunge her in right down at the end of your trail. What could be better to heal your horse with than all that fresh salt air and turning her out on that nice, firm, sandy surface. To tone up her muscles in equal proportions you would hold the lunge line in one hand, the lunge whip in the other, then let the horse run so many times in one direction, then so many times in the other. It also teaches them how to change leads."

"It sounds like a good plan," she agreed. "What else would her treatment entail?"

"It seems logical to me to take advantage of one of the most natural healing sources in the world - saltwater," he was warming to the subject more and more as the plan took shape in his mind.

"It's an ingenious idea," she enthused.

"Well, the salt would be good for her hooves and legs. Working her out in the surf would force her to lift up her hind legs with each step. In turn both would help to strengthen the damaged cartilage and develop her atrophied muscles."

"You make it sound so possible, almost inevitable," Helmi said with genuine sincerity.

"What could be more rewarding than to witness the progress of a beautiful creature like Windflower to reach her full potential," he replied, pleased with her obvious interest in the project.

"You're so knowledgeable and experienced in these matters. You seem to be the perfect candidate for the job. Would you be willing to work with us in your spare time?" she asked knowing full well that it was a lot to expect but also that he was her only hope.

"I guess I should have known that would be the next question," he said with a wink. "I don't really have all that much spare time, but you can bet any I can find will be yours."

"I would be forever indebted to you," she said, the relief plain in her voice.

"Yes you would be," he said, his eyes flashing. "And I would be the first one to keep you constantly reminded of it."

"It's a deal then?" she held out her hand for the gentleman's shake.

"You've got yourself one hell of a deal," he said, bending to press his lips to her outstretched hand as he grasped it.

She felt her cheeks flushing but didn't hurry to withdraw her hand from the warm, dry haven of his.

His gesture, though completely spontaneous, caused both of them to squirm and Helmi thought she detected a slight blush in his cheeks. They both knew he wasn't in the habit of kissing a woman's hand.

Still she felt flattered that he'd done it, secretly wishing he would do much more than that.

Guessing her fleeting thoughts as he raised his eyes to hers, he searched their depths for more glimpses into the promise they held.

But the moment had passed and the impenetrable veil that he'd become familiar with was firmly in place once more, denying him entry into her soul's core.

They resumed their discussion of Windflower's special handling and the order by which its sequential steps would proceed.

"Whenever I can finish my ranch chores early I'll head over here and work with Windflower. It could be as much as three hours a day several days a week," he suggested. "First I'll lunge her on the beach and get her used to the various gaits, then proceed to saddling and bridling her and finally, breaking her in for riding. After she's done all that, and proficient in each area, we can begin the saltwater therapy."

"I can hardly wait to get started," Helmi said.

"One important point we have to keep in mind is that just because you're breaking in a horse to ride doesn't mean that you have to break its spirit," Knute warned. "My system is very slow and gradual so that they hardly know they're being tamed. It's more a matter of months, sometimes even years, rather than days or weeks."

"I like the principle behind your methodology. It sounds very humane and at the same time so effective," she replied gratefully.

"That's the general idea," he said. "The less pain and discomfort the trainer causes, the more cooperative and receptive to learning new things the animal becomes. There are no short-cuts in horse training."

"When would you like to start with her?" Helmi asked, hoping he was as anxious as she to begin.

"The sooner the better," he said, sensing her impatience to set the horse on the planned course of action.

"That's fine with me," she replied. "Yes, I definitely agree. It's past time for Windflower to begin working on a full recovery."

"Just wait and see," he reassured her confidently. "You'll be a witness to one
spectacular comeback."

"And her coming of age too," she added, with a touch of triumph to her tone, "all happening at the same time."

"She's definitely worth all the trouble you're prepared to go to for her sake," he said. "She has near perfect conformation and her tri-colored brown, white and copper markings, with black stockings, mane and tail, are extremely rare. She would probably produce exquisite, loud-colored foals if you decided to breed her."

"That would be a dream come true," she sighed wistfully. "I never dared hope that anything like it could be possible."

"Better get used to it," he said with finality. "One of the things that would give me the most pleasure in the whole world would be to make a dream of yours come true."

The desire in his eyes was unmistakable. Suddenly he had exalted her to some secret, lofty pedestal.

"How very gallant," she said a trifle flippantly, trying to lighten up the moment. She was slightly startled by the intensity with which he had spoken.

Though he didn't emote often, the depth of his feelings was undeniable.

Before he left her they agreed to meet the following Saturday afternoon so he could begin working with Windflower.

Once more, as he left, he threw her a look of such abject longing that her heart did strange little flip-flops.

Again, caught off-guard, she stifled her own emotions by standing calmly watching his every move with her eyes like a hunted animal.

As much as she wanted him she had no intention of becoming entrapped.

He saw her stiffen slightly. No matter how sensitive or deliberate his pursuit of her, his instincts warned him she would, like a stalked wild thing, always protect her elemental freedom.

He sensed she felt something for him but he also knew that he would have to proceed cautiously. Whatever her past relationship, he thought, it had definitely left a deep-seeded scar in its wake.

And then he was gone. She felt a sudden sense of loss.

He came soon after she had finished breakfast Saturday morning. They drank their ritual cup of coffee together until he became restless to begin his work.

She decided it would be better to allow him adequate time to get acquainted with Windflower before she joined them. She knew she could always observe most of the activity from the safe distance of the house.

She saw that he had taken the lead rope, lunge line and whip from the tack room and was walking Windflower into the pasture.

Windflower was nervously pawing the ground while at the same time dancing a little jig in a tight circle around Knute. He gave her as much head as he possibly could without endangering himself. She was extremely tense and agitated, not entirely sure how much she could trust what he was up to. He could tell she remembered him by the way she sniffed him more like a friendly puppy than a frightened filly. He liked her alert, curious nature. A good sign, he thought to himself, while also at the same time foreseeing that she would undoubtedly be a quick study. The native intelligence smoldering in her deep brown eyes assured him of that. He noted again to himself that this was no ordinary horse. She had all the necessary qualities that earmarked her for great things to come.

She was watching him intently, somehow catching his meaning as he murmured under his breath to himself.

"Mark my words, you are going to be a star when I'm finished with you. You didn't know that I have big plans for you did you girl?"

But then gazing once again into those huge, soulful eyes he was certain that she knew.

"Now let's get to work, shall we?" he proposed.

He led her out to the center of the lower section of the pasture where there was a level, circular area. Gradually he let out the slack in the lunge line until she was quite a considerable distance from where he stood. Taking up the lunge whip in the other hand he gently encouraged her to move at a walk to the left. Whenever she slowed up or turned out he lifted the whip and moved it to her rear; never touching her but keeping it circling rhythmically where she could see it out of the corner of her eye.

She took to it with the natural ease he knew she would. And she took it stride for stride with style and grace, as if she had been born to it.

He could see that she favored slightly the one badly injured side, where the muscles of that thigh weren't as well developed as the other thigh. It was almost as though she depended on the healthy leg so totally that the damaged one had not grown in quite the same way or even at the same rate.

She walked with a kind of sashay. Her hips rolled from side to side. It was as if the one leg hadn't reached the same level of maturity as the other and had some catching up to do before it would even be the exact same length.

He had her walk in the opposite direction, which was not as much to her liking. But his soothing voice urged her on while the lunge whip kept her in line and moving.

As he eased her into a trot, her gait smoothed out somewhat which he had expected and knew to be the case in certain kinds of injuries. Her trot soon became high-stepping and prance-like. She held her head and tail proud and erect. It was obvious she was enjoying herself. Around and around she went, first in one direction, then the other.

"So you think you're pretty hot stuff do you?" he needled her. "One thing is for sure. You are a show-off. There's no doubt about that."

She seemed to be taking so well and quickly to the lunge line that he decided to step up the pace.

"Canter," he called out to her in a low, firm voice just at the moment he moved closer to her and snapped the whip on the ground behind her.

Momentarily startled she stumbled slightly as she changed leads in preparation for the faster pace. She charged forward with abandon, instantly responsive to his commands. Her canter was even more fluid and lyrical than her trot.

"OK,OK" he laughed, hanging on to the stretched line with all his might, "so you like to go fast. I get the message. But let's see if you can do as well in the opposite direction. Stretch and extend those back legs. That's it. You need to tone up those flabby muscles."

Her ears were pricked forward alertly, listening intently to every word he spoke, sometimes anticipating his thoughts before he uttered them.

Her reflexes were swift as lightning. She was even more promising, with more potential, than he had previously imagined.

And on top of all that she was one of the most exquisite creatures he had ever seen.

Helmi joined them midway through their morning workout.

"How are you two getting along?" she asked reluctantly, fearing his prognosis may be worse than she supposed. "Famously, from what I could see from the house."

"Better than I dared dream could be possible," he confessed, clearly relieved. "She's definitely got a mind of her own but those kind make the best riding horses if they're handled properly. More spirited which translates into more of a challenge."

"One thing I've never worried about Windflower was whether she would be a challenge. I can hardly wait to ride her, from what I've seen so far. She looks like she'll be exhilarating."

"She will be as soon as she gets the hang of the different gaits," he replied. "Right now she's pretty rough around the edges, needs constant handling and discipline. Only a very experienced rider should be allowed on her at this stage. This ground work should prove to be a very crucial phase of her training. It could make her or break her in terms of her becoming a quality pleasure riding horse."

"I have full confidence in your horsemanship skills," she assured him. "I'm sure, under your tutelage, she'll turn out to be one of the best, most versatile horses around."

"You are too kind," he feigned mock modesty. "But it is a little early to forecast the future for my star pupil."

"I'm very optimistic, though, and you are too, aren't you?" she prodded.

"I want to be but it is still too soon to tell. I need time to make more inroads into the Windflower mystique."

"You can have all the time you want as far as that goes," she said. "I'm in no hurry. I can see where it would be beneficial to her to go gradually."

"We'll work on her pace in the various gaits for a few more weeks and then try lunging her down on the beach in the compact sand," he explained, mapping out his initial strategy. "That will be the best therapy we can give her as she slowly strengthens her muscles."

"I always thought that had to be the greatest workout arena in existence," she agreed.

"Consider it done then," he told her, watching her face as it softened with relief.

"When you finish working her out and doing the stable chores why don't you come and join me for drinks and an early dinner?"

"That sounds like the best idea I've heard in a long time. You're on."

"OK. Good. I'll go in and start getting things organized in preparation for the arrival of the West's greatest wild horse tamer," she called over her shoulder as she headed back toward the house. "Such esteemed company I so rarely have the privilege to entertain."

"Better get used to it," he laughingly called after her. Which he knew they were both going to enjoy doing exceedingly well.

He and the mare worked out together awhile longer. He urged her around and around in a circular configuration again and again, first in one direction and then in the other. He could see she loved speed and did not appear to notice, or allow in the least, her injury to hamper her. She was an exquisite sight to behold, her black mane and tail flying out behind her as she cantered, seemingly laughing, into the wind. Slowing to a halt she gave a satisfied snort, her nostrils flaring, her eyes flashing.

"Take it easy girl," Knute said in a low, calming voice. "You act as though you're training for a major league stakes race. What are you getting yourself so worked up about? Here, now, you're all lathered up into a sweaty mess. We'll have to call it a day and let you cool off. We're just trying to get you ready for me to saddle up and ride you." Speaking in a low, constant, singsong tone as he led her to the hitching post, he brushed away the sweat. "Let's go in and get you fed and watered," he said and she whickered her approval. He then threw a thin turnout sheet over her to insure she didn't catch a chill.

"Remember, don't drink too much water until you've cooled down quite a bit more," he cautioned her with the familiar way that she had come to understand instantly. "We'll pick up again here when I come back in another few days. Good work girl. Keep it up," were the words he left her with as he turned toward the house and Helmi who was waiting for him with cold drinks.

She handed him a glass of vodka. "I know you usually like beer but I thought I'd introduce you to my drink of choice." Her warm, hospitable manner became her and impressed him greatly.

"So you're a hard-drinking martini girl," he teased.

"Yes," she replied with a twinkle in her eye, "if you call a glass three quarters full of sparkling water hard-drinking."

"So that's the key to your fountain of youth is it? Russian vodka and bubbly water." He was genuinely intrigued as to the possible source of her youthful vitality. She always radiated a healthy inner glow.

"That and good genes. I had two sets of very long-lived grandparents who taught me well by their example of working hard and playing even harder," she told him.

"I can identify more with the playing hard part," he admitted, although she knew he was merely being modest and that he was an extremely industrious worker.

"They loved to throw big parties out at their farm in Riverside," she said. "I have many memories of festive times out there and that they were a very popular host and hostess. Their graciousness and hospitality were legendary among their friends."

Knute was sipping his drink with relish, noting that she put hardly any mixer in his. He'd heard of martinis, but this was the first he'd had and was already starting to feel it.

"A potentially dangerous and potent potion," he thought to himself.

"What are you grinning about?" she asked, again noticing the secretive, mysterious smile spread slowly over his face.

"Oh nothing. Just thinking about how good I feel. All warm and expansive inside. This stuff is dynamite for bringing a repressed guy out of his shell," he confessed somewhat sheepishly.

"It was the drink of choice for all the Czars," she said with just a hint of pride in her voice, adding, " it is also the Rolls Royce of all the vodkas. One of my few splurges in life, a treat to myself, but definitely worth it."

"God, is it good, so smooth and pure," he agreed. "I could drink about ten of these easily."

"Go easy, sip slowly and you'll be fine. But be careful. It can sneak up on you if you let it," she said giving him one of her friendly 'pearls of wisdom'.

"I've been duly forewarned," he laughed. "But you're the one I should caution that I'm beginning to feel something. Amorous is the word I'm looking for, I believe."

"I'll take my chances. Maybe that was the precise effect I had in mind," she said.

"A premeditated method to your madness in other words?" he needled softly.

"Exactly. How perceptive you are," she taunted.

She brought out the tray of hors d'oeuvres she had prepared - jumbo prawns with her own homemade cocktail sauce. There was also a plate of raw vegetables with dip and another of cheese and crackers. She was hoping at least one of them would be to his taste but had no idea how well she had succeeded.

"Prawns. My favorite," he said, the delight plain on his face. "How did you know?"

"Just a wild guess," she replied, obviously flattered by his pleasure. "They're not local, though. I had to go clear over to the Tokeson fish processing plant to get them. It's nice to see them appreciated. I love them, too. Can't ever seem to get my fill of them."

"I know a cannery near this area, in Cambray, that sells local shrimp. But they're not nearly as large as these or necessarily any better," he said.

"It might be worth a try if it's closer and they sell them fresh. I'd like to go there and check it out someday," she told him.

I have several friends in commercial fishing. It would be a cinch to arrange anytime you'd like to go," he replied.

"I'm always in the market for good, fresh seafood," she said. "Whenever we can both get away at the same time, let's do it."

"Sounds like a good plan to me," he said. "I love it, too. It would be a great way to see a sampling of the various fish available in this area, like the oysters, Walamath Bay clams and last but by no means least, the Pacific razor clams.

Speaking in between bites he systematically popped one prawn after the other into his mouth, using his teeth to pull it out of its tail.

Watching his enjoyment made her hungry and she did the same.

After awhile he poured them another drink, following her ratio, while she set the table and started the dinner. She was fixing fried chicken and potato salad, a couple of her specialties from old recipes handed down by her grandmother.

The delicious aromas wafting from the sizzling frying pan and full mixing bowl made his mouth water. He felt a twinge of awe at the deftness with which she moved, feline-like, around the kitchen, stirring, turning, bending and stretching. It was, for him, like watching a well-executed rodeo event, without one awkward or wasted maneuver.

It was beginning to dawn on Knute, feeling the same way he did when working with Windflower, the immense enjoyment he derived from watching her. To him she symbolized infinite grace and beauty. A wild spirit, an exquisitely born being - mysterious, magical and poetic. He did not know what it was about her. He could not define the ethereal, the ephemeral essence of her that so intrigued him.

She felt his eyes following her. At first the intensity of his gaze unnerved her. But slowly she let herself unwind, began to unfold under the spell of his evident enchantment.

"Dinner will be ready in a few minutes," she announced

from the dining room where she was putting the finishing touches on the table. A bouquet of wild field flowers arranged loosely in a colorful pottery vase served as the centerpiece. "Freshen up your drink and bring it to the table if you'd like. Touch mine up too would you please? It's there on the counter."

Knute was happy to oblige, feeling mellower and freer than he had for a long while. His solitary existence hadn't groomed him to socialize but he was soon drawn to it instinctively, a revelation he rather relished.

The tabletop, he noted, was covered with richly-colored pottery. The dinnerware pieces were hand-painted with various animals against a festive assortment of background colors. So warm and inviting a setting was it that he gravitated naturally to it in a mood both bemused and buoyant. Beeswax candles glowed on either side of the flowers, infusing everything with a radiant glow.

"Let's be seated," she motioned him to one end of the long pine table with a wave of her arm.

He surprised her by coming over to hold her chair for her as she sat down. Noticing her startled expression, he further undid her by saying, "I wasn't born in a barn, you know, though pretty close to it."

"You never have told me that much about yourself. Please fill me in," she probed. She could see that he was reluctant to talk about himself, but the drinks had loosened his tongue dramatically.

"I was born and raised in central Oregon. It was on the outskirts of a reservation. My dad always claimed I'm part Native American myself and I wouldn't doubt it," he said hotly, "but there wasn't ever any definite proof. All I remember is that the conditions surrounding my childhood weren't the best. In fact they were downright disgusting. It seemed to me we lived more like half-starved animals than human beings. We were poverty-stricken, you might say, in the early years until I could get odd jobs to help out."

"Conditions were so difficult for you," Helmi said, feeling genuine dismay. "What did you do after those years of hardship?"

"I moved to eastern Oregon. Before I started working for the BLM I got myself a job as a ranch hand on a big spread. I learned to ride expertly. You had to or you were out of luck," he recalled, "and that worked into herding livestock. By the way this chicken tastes great. Reminds me of the ranch food we used to get when we came in after riding out on the range all day."

"Thanks. It's almost as good as grandmother's," she said, relieved not to have overcooked it. "I'm beginning to see now why you're so good with horses, so skillful at training them. That ranch job and life out in the wilderness turned out to be invaluable experience. You gained knowledge in those few years, before you came here that would take most people a lifetime to acquire."

Her eyes were aglow with admiration and that dark something that told of feelings delving far deeper than that. The heat of her emotional outburst caused in him a slight stir of embarrassment. But his eyes held an answering echo as well. It was as if, at that exact moment, his spirit was rising and going to meet hers half way.

"And you never married nor had a family?" she prodded him to further revelations.

But he was expecting the unintentional prying and chose to counteract it with a succinct reply, "No, I never did. Never had the time or the inclination. And not the opportunity either for that matter. What about you?"

"I'm afraid I didn't escape quite as easily as you did," she sighed somewhat wistfully. "It was a long time ago, so long that I can only vaguely remember the sordid details, thankfully."

"So it was that bad, was it?" he asked, serving himself another helping of potato salad. "I guess I'm not too surprised, but sorry you had to suffer. What was the trouble?" he encouraged her by his gentle tone to confide in him.

She watched his features sag into a compassionate softness as he waited for her to continue. It had been so long since she had spoken of the past that she groped for a place to begin.

"I was very young and impulsive," she began in a small, faraway voice as she traveled back in time to that painful place. "I thought I was madly, passionately in love but it was more with the idea of love than with the person. I didn't know him very well. It turned out to be a catastrophic mistake."

"Why was that?" Knute asked, noticing that she was beginning to open to the cathartic experience of exorcising that unhappy period of her life by confessing it.

"It started well enough, quite romantically actually, but quickly went downhill from there. I knew after only a few weeks that it wasn't going to work."

"How so?" Knute wanted to know.

"Mostly because I didn't want it to. I just couldn't see how to make it work. After all, there were so many fundamental differences between us, religion mostly. I just couldn't reconcile myself to them. Our tastes and interests were so different, not to mention backgrounds, educations and temperaments."

"Whoa. Hold up there. You're getting way ahead of me," Knute jokingly begged her. "Was he cruel to you, or abusive?"

"I'd say yes definitely, at least psychologically abusive. Neglect was a major part of the whole relationship. He was the coldest, most emotionally repressed individual I've ever known. In almost six years together I hardly received any affection at all. He didn't know how to show feeling and I didn't know how to survive without it. Also we were very financially strapped for most of the time.

Knute could see by the strained set of her face that she'd been to the depths of despair during that devastating time. He wanted only to comfort and protect her from further hurt. He also knew it would be therapeutic for her to release her pent-up anguish.

"Go on," he said quietly, knowing by this time she was intent on making sense of what happened. She was hardly aware of his presence.

As if in a trance, she spoke barely above a whisper," I don't think I ever really loved him. I don't know if I ever knew who he really was or if he even knew himself. There was always a very dark, mysterious part of him he kept completely to himself. No, it was as if he were an unformed entity completely at my disposal to mold into anything I desired. And that's exactly what I did. It was my imagination's conjured creation that I fell in love with, not the actual man."

"But he loved you desperately, was that it?" Knute asked.

"That is what everybody around us seemed to believe. At least that he did in the beginning. Until he could see how unhappy and ill I was becoming. But even worse than the problems just between the two of us, were the problems his family posed for us. They were wonderful in the beginning or so I blindly thought, until all of our troubles surfaced. It was then that I saw them for what they really were, a blood-sucking school of sharks, coming in for the kill, a feeding frenzy over the carcass of a dying marriage."

All in all, Helmi smiled to herself the next morning while thinking about the previous night, *it had turned out to be a lovely evening.* As she stood before her bathroom mirror applying her make-up she relived each precious minute. Knute could not have been more charming as a dinner companion. At different moments he had displayed signs of thoughtfulness, sensitivity, astuteness and wit. But more importantly, he had been a good listener. He had listened with his whole heart. And he had genuinely seemed to care. It was a deep, untainted kind of love he held out to her as if on a silver platter, a glorious feast offering as sumptuous as pheasant under glass.

Thank heaven, she thought, *he didn't muck everything up by making premature physical overtures.* She just did not feel ready to be that completely involved yet. She gave so deeply of herself that she would have to feel very sure of her terrain before going further. Lately, things seemed to be falling into place to the point where it was beginning to feel safe for her to proceed. Together she and Knute had carefully laid the groundwork for their future like an intricately tiled mosaic design. But the pattern was that of a maze which they would have to patiently traverse to the point of completion.

When Knute arrived the following Tuesday for Windflower's next workout session, he appeared completely calm and nonchalant with no mention of their recent evening together. Nor did Helmi mention it. But she knew in her heart that they had made tremendous inroads toward a closer bond and greater intimacy in their relationship.

Knute's plan, after several months of ground training both in the pasture and on the beach, was to saddle Windflower up for riding. She had just turned two, the usual age a young horse is broken in or started under saddle. Any sooner and their bone structure is not fully developed and could be permanently damaged.

He led her to the hitching post and loosely tied her. Then he took the saddle blanket and began very slowly and deliberately rubbing it over her back and withers, then along either side of her neck, her underbelly and down over her shoulders, then each of her legs and even her tail. He wanted her to be fully accustomed to the feel of material and equipment touching her sides and belly. This he did patiently and methodically over and over. At first she seemed agitated by the unfamiliar feeling and danced restlessly from side to side. Knute kept up his continuous singsong chanting softly in her ear which seemed gradually to have a calming effect on her. Very slowly she settled down and allowed Knute to place the blanket over her back and let it rest easily there. He kept all of his movements extremely quiet as he worked. Soon he reached for the saddle straddling the wood railing, slowly raised it and swung it over her back, careful not to let the girth strap or stirrups slap against her sides. She snorted and stepped suddenly sideways with the extra weight. She'd never known anything like this before in her life and didn't know quite what to make of it. By stroking her gently and whispering to her softly Knute soon had soothed her to the point where she was ready for the next step.

Helmi, awed and amazed, watched the entire proceedings from the large picture window in the dining room. She had decided that if she stayed at a distance it would be less distracting for Windflower and easier for Knute to have her undivided attention. From what Helmi could see they seemed to have formed some rare and special bond. Windflower was responding to his slightest touch and voice commands with telepathic sensitivity. He seemed to have gained her complete confidence and trust.

It would take every ounce of that and more in readying her to take the bit. He decided to wait on that stage and just use the halter and two lead ropes, one on either side, as temporary reins. Teaching a horse to neck rein, for Knute, had always been an extremely crucial procedure, one taking infinite finesse and patience. It also happened to be one of his specialties, one in which he thoroughly enjoyed seeing his horse excel.

He could tell already that Windflower would be a natural in this particular discipline. She responded to the slightest pressure he applied as he pulled the left rope gently toward her right side. She quickly arched her neck gracefully to the right and followed that movement up by a series of strides in the same direction. Knute was astounded by the deftness with which she executed the new exercise. It was like a game to her, as if she had been neck reining all her life. She pranced with pleasure, head and tail held high, as Knute stroked her over and over, cooing and making a great fuss over her new-found prowess.

In order that it would be second nature to her, he directed her to try it again and again, to the left for awhile, then the right, then alternating. Every so often he would pull her up and, gently tugging on both ropes simultaneously, would ask her to step back.

"Back, back. That's it girl, you've got it," he cried excitedly. "Let's go again. Back, back and back and whoa. Good girl. You did it."

Going backwards seemed to be her favorite thing that she'd learned so far. But he knew from many hours of observing her that running full out for all she was worth would always be what she was born to do.

Where her desire to run came from Knute was not sure he would ever know. It was not a characteristic usually associated with her breed. Strength and endurance were traits more in keeping with her kind. He thought it might have something to do more with her spirit. A spirit she possessed almost exclusively owing to the love and devotion Helmi had showered on her ever since she'd known her.

But what was unmistakable was the fact that she was a natural born athlete. From what he had observed, she could be or do just about anything she was asked to be or do. Probably she could even be a racehorse if she were trained to be one. Yet Helmi was asking nothing more of her than that she be a good pleasure-trail riding horse and a good companion. She was, Knute knew, already well on her way to excelling in both of those arenas. She was turning out to far exceed all of their wildest dreams regarding her potential. With regular workouts and continuous therapeutic treatments he knew deep in his heart that, without doubt, she was going to be a star.

But what was most surprising to him of all, since he had begun working with her, was how much he had grown to care for her and her well-being.

She already had a very pronounced character and a unique personality to go with it. A feisty streak? Yes. But not in a malicious vein, rather having more of a playful flavor. Her overall nature was sociable, affectionate and extremely loving. The way she interacted almost humanly with Helmi - following her every move with those trusting doe-like eyes - was inspiring to Knute. Something he had never, to that degree, born witness to before.

The following week he was back with Helmi and Windflower at Wildwood, impatient to begin the next workout.

He led the mare out of her stall and to the hitching post for saddling, all the while observing how much calmer she was, not only to lead, but in her general demeanor. No longer did she toss her head and thrash, wild-eyed, whenever he, the stranger approached. Instead her behavior seemed to improve day by day as if she were consciously striving to better herself. She moved like she knew she was somehow special and being groomed for something special, she knew not what, that she was fully going to master.

Knute reveled in her newly cooperative spirit, as refreshing to him as if he were splashing in the pool of a mountain waterfall.

The most difficult part of the gentling process was clearly behind them. From then on it would be building upon the foundation they had established, patiently, consistently and slowly.

He was anxious to get started on something he hadn't yet tried with her. It was an age-old therapy useful in the rehabilitation of injured horses. He not only knew of its beneficial healing properties but had become highly proficient in it as part of his work with the BLM's horses.

After saddling Windflower, all the while talking soothingly to her in a kind of soft chant, he led her slowly to the beach trail head and mounted. She stood relatively still, only pacing slightly back and forth as he lowered into the saddle.

It had been almost a week since he had taken her out and she was displaying the earmarks of restlessness that inactivity engenders.

With a few short stomps and snorts she settled down and, pricking her ears forward alertly, let Knute know she was raring to go.

He was just as antsy as she to get going. Their mutual excitement was like an electrical circuit moving back and forth between them. For a few moments they treaded, dancing in place, until Knute spurred her on by gently squeezing each of her sides with his knees.

She moved forward gracefully, trotting up the incline to gather momentum, then slowed to a walk the rest of the way along the grassy path to the beach.

Her nostrils heaved at the first whiff of sea air and her body rippled in eagerness to jog through the dunes, until finally reaching the warm sand.

She loved the sea. That was clear by the spring in her step and the lilting little leaps she took in the deep dry depths. It was as if she had come home. The place where she craved to smell the tangy sea scents and lap up the ethereal moodiness as she had been doing from the first moment she had come to live with Helmi, and Knute had begun to work with her.

Knute edged her closer to the water's edge slowly so as not to alarm her. She had only been near it, never in it. It had to be a gradual introduction - to the shock of the cold, the motion of the waves, the shifting patterns of the sand. He wanted her to feel the ocean as her friend, not some cruel sea monster about to swallow her up.

So far his efforts looked like they were paying off. She appeared to love the water. *After all,* Knute smiled to himself, *she was born in the month of Pisces. She's a regular fish.*

She stepped gingerly into the surf and quickly recoiled, like a rattlesnake striking its prey. She snorted, startled, shook and shivered until Knute felt like he was being bounced around in a washing machine. What a weird sensation, he thought, like the times I tossed coins in the slot, hopped on top of the bucking wooden horse in the penny arcade and let her rip. Everything jiggled violently back and forth, up and down, until he thought he would go on ricocheting forever or be sick. Of course neither happened but he never forgot the sensation.

They walked slowly, step by tentative step, along the edge of the surf, until she felt more familiar with the terrain. As the larger waves broke onto the shore, she was forced to lift her back legs higher in an effort to step through them. The deeper they ventured out the more rigorous the stepping action became and the more strenuously the injured hind leg was massaged and exercised.

She was beginning to enjoy the treatment. It was already

becoming a kind of exhilarating game; a challenge to be constantly on the alert for dangerous pitfalls.

Well into the workout, she and most of the tack were soaked. For a change of pace, Knute steered her toward the shore. The hard-packed sandy surface was a perfect outdoor arena, the best part being its lack of constraints. As far as he knew it was the only riding track in the world that ran beside the sea for thirty miles without a single obstacle.

It is the ideal setting for training Windflower who is already showing a marked dislike of boundaries of any sort. Her nature is as synonymous with freedom as her namesake. She will never submit to being completely tamed. Bonding is transpiring gradually, but total surrender will never be likely. She is a thing of nature, of the elements, at one with the wild beauty - of the forest, sea and sky. She can be owned, she can be trained, but never totally possessed. Her spirit will always remain free, just as she will remain deep, mysterious, endlessly intriguing.

Knute introduced her to the different paces and they carved out a figure eight pattern in which to walk, trot and canter. He started slowly, talking quietly all the while, encouraging her to assume the correct lead, gait, position and rhythm. He urged her to relax, stretch and fully extend her hind legs. And then, as the sun began to sink toward the horizon, he pulled her up and headed for the trail. She was breathing hard, had worked up a noticeable sweat and seemed relieved to be going in. Knute relished her rapid progress and the discipline and intensity she displayed during their session. She seemed genuinely interested and willing to tackle every new problem he presented, remaining relatively undaunted.

He foresaw a productive future for her at the rate she was advancing. He was also gratified to learn how manageable she was going to be. Best of all, though, was how passionately she threw herself into whatever was put before her. He had worked with few horses with that same degree of vitality. To his mind she was becoming somewhat of a phenomenon and he was curious to see the end result.

After they got back to the ranch, Knute put away the tack, brushed her down, carefully removing the sweaty residue, and then brought out the liniment oil. Very gently he rubbed it into her hips, flanks and up and down her back legs. She kept trying to move away from the cold shock of it, but he continued applying pressure firmly over her hindquarters. Again and again he massaged the soothing liquid into her coat and skin with his fingertips until he could feel the tenseness of her muscles relax and the knots recede. With time, patience and constant ministrations, Knute was confident that her limbs would be strengthened, supple and ultimately sound. He also knew the time and effort it would take and the amount of work that lay before them.

Week after week, Knute put Windflower through the rigors of the saltwater therapy that had become his specialty since he had begun working with horses. Week after week he watched as the sea injected its magical healing properties into her injured tendons, muscles, bones and, for all Knute knew, possible other areas not even he was aware of. She was responding well and thriving in spite of her initial skepticism. They ventured more deeply into the surf every outing. There the pressure of the waves pounded rhythmically against the affected limbs like a masseuse kneading the tired muscles of a prizefighter. The ebb and flow motion swirling around them stimulated the atrophied section, pumping nutrients into every pore.

Windflower was gaining so much lost ground that by the end of the first several months of treatment, Helmi began to consider working her out herself.

Knute was extremely supportive of the idea, encouraging her and actively trying to boost her confidence.

"She is completely trained for voice commands," he told her. "You just have to be firm with her, let her know who's boss and what you want her to do. She's an easily controllable horse, so you really have nothing to worry about. And she's almost all the way back to one hundred percent."

The next thing Helmi knew, Knute had her in the saddle, leading them to the trail and walking along behind them as they headed to the beach.

It was an exhilarating feeling for Helmi to be back in the saddle. Windflower felt like she fit underneath her like a glove to her hand. Her conformation was a superb match for Helmi's size and weight. Their proportions were perfectly suited to each other.

Knute, watching them from behind, was impressed. "You look like you were born in the saddle," he marveled. And when Windflower, in her excitement, began trotting, Helmi moved with her in sync, barely budging from her seat. Knute couldn't help remarking, "You two move together as if you are one."

Helmi couldn't help feeling proud of herself, but especially of her horse. She was beautiful, spirited and graceful and Helmi noticed something else - her new-found confidence in her own abilities and proficiency.

> *Prowess is more like it,* she mused. *She slinks through this wild sea grass like a stalking jungle cat, completely at home, in tune with and aware of her powers. Today she seems more like a panther than a horse. What is also obvious is that she is going to make an excellent trail riding horse. The Indians knew what they were doing when they chose her breed - horses known for their endurance, strength and stamina. Someday we will undertake an adventurous foray out into the wilderness where we will both be in our element.*

They had almost reached the beach when Windflower suddenly broke into a trot up the hill above the dunes. They crossed the soft sand section then trotted again once they hit the firmer ground of hard-packed sand next to the shore.

"When she goes into a trot," Helmi laughed back over her shoulder to Knute who was trying to catch up, "her gait is so smooth that it feels like we're floating."

Knute could see what Helmi could feel - that they were made for each other - that all the months of closeness, the hours together before they began riding - had forged an indelible bond between horse and rider. Their bodies melded together seamlessly and as they gathered speed it felt as if they were about to take off and soar into space.

....

PART IV

All the while Knute had been working with Windflower, Helmi had been overseeing the remodeling of the guesthouse.

The small cabin down the road from the main house was literally disintegrating into the ground when she decided to undertake the project. The Baylors had left it in a nasty state of disrepair. Between the army of insects ingesting large portions of the wooden frame and walls and the huge degree of dry-rot, the structure was barely salvageable.

A seedy carpet glued to old fir floors permeated the air with the stench of mildew. Many of the appliances were either rusted out or inoperable. Filth and mold were pervasive and adding to the dank, depressing atmosphere was the lack of adequate light.

When Helmi first saw the inside, she shivered in revulsion. Her skin felt like it was crawling with vermin as she walked through the tiny, musty rooms. And yet, even then, she could see the possibilities, that what little charm and character it did possess could be enhanced. It definitely had potential, she decided, and nothing could deter her.

No matter who came along, no one ever had much hope for the old shack. "It must be at least seventy five years old," someone said. "It's seen its better days. What's there to save?" "Why not tear it down and start over?" said someone else. "It would save you money in the long run."

Typical, Helmi muttered to herself, *of the attitude of just about everyone who stops by for a visit. There seems to be an epidemic of naysayers sweeping this area like the disease infesting the spruce trees. It is a mystery to me how this paradise we live in attracts people with such an ugly streak of pessimism. I wonder. Could it be weather-related? The oppressive cloud cover, blocking any sunshine, seems not only to alter moods but debilitate souls as well.*

She liked the patina of certain old things, the mellowness that aged wood achieved that could not be found in the new. She loved the imperfections in the pane-glass windows and the solid purity of old porcelain sinks and tubs. These few treasures, still intact in the cottage, were, for her, worth all the expenditure - of time, money and the back-breaking labor it would entail to restore it over the next months.

And so, with Knute thoroughly ensconced in Windflower's rehabilitation, Helmi braced herself for a thorough renovation of what she considered to be her tiny jewel box in the woods.

She hired a local architect with whom she would collaborate, using all the design skills she had acquired restoring her previous houses in the city.

In this arena, she was in her element. She knew space, proportion and materials better than almost anything else. She thrived with the challenge building decision-making presented. Whether to patch or replace insect-damaged, dry-rotted exterior walls? What about raising the entire structure a foot-and-a-half out of the dirt? To substitute posts and beams with cement blocks or replace damaged areas? Exchange existing clapboard exterior for cedar shingles or repair what was there? New carpet or refinish old fir floors? What kind of heat, lighting fixtures, tile, paint and appliances? She was constantly consulted by the architect, crew, sub-contractors and suppliers.

Every day from morning until dinner she was caught up in a flurry of plans, advice, deadlines and deliveries. She was thoroughly absorbed, exhausted and exhilarated. At times the sheer volume of details for which she was responsible was simply overwhelming. But all the while she bore witness to her vision coming into being. She watched as the little house that had lain dormant for so long emerged into the light, endowed with new life, as warm as the welcome of outstretched arms.

Over the long months of its transformation, the guest quarters had gone through various phases. There was the initial tear-out stage where everything was gutted until nothing but the outer shell remained. And that was largely riddled with rot and the detritus left behind by deserted insects.

Then there was the reconstruction stage where walls, beams, studs and panels were replaced or added. In order to elevate a sagging section of the roofline, a huge beam was installed from which a support wall was created. It ran along the elbow of the L-shaped main room out of which grew two rooms with a wide doorway between. The smaller room became a tiny sleeping alcove off of which was an even tinier laundry room.

What was once the front porch became the dining room needing salvaged fir planks to match the other vintage flooring. Old boards of phenomenal similarity were finally found across the river and installed by Sam Hellstrom, the construction foreman.
From there they put up new sheet-rock in the dining room and kitchen, the latter also outfitted with ready-made blonde wood cabinets and maple counter-tops. A few small-paned, wood framed windows needed replacing, though they were able to retain most of the originals.

A small front porch was fashioned out of clear cedar strips and peeled lodge-poles supported the overhang.

Finally the exterior and roof were freshly clad in cedar shingles. Helmi watched, day after day, as the crew hammered one at a time by hand, row after row until she thought she would expire from impatience. For her, it was the most exasperating, and also the most satisfying aspect of the whole project. The time it took to nail on those shingles made her feel frustrated out of a year of her life. But ultimately, all the added expense was worth every cent of extra effort.

With the last stage came the period of her greatest personal involvement, challenge and enjoyment. It was the time of richest rewards when things began to fall into place at last. With the finishing touches, she could see the final results. The floors were sanded and polished until they gleamed. The walls and woodwork whitewashed. The shiny new fixtures were set in place and the antique ones cleaned and whitened. Hand-glazed, imported tiles were carefully set in place in the bath enclosure and the rest of the room wrapped in cedar to lend a sauna-like atmosphere. The same earthy tiles made up the kitchen counter back-splash, adding a rustic touch.

The centerpiece of the living room became the tiny, used-brick fireplace. Recently fitted with an antique pine mantle of perfect proportions, it lent the key ingredient for a quintessentially cozy beach cabin.

A wood-paddled ceiling fan added a tropical touch. And small-paned casement windows on either side of the fireplace not only increased the flow of fresh air but let in much needed additional light as well.

But best of all to Helmi was the challenge of scouting out unique pieces for the space's various nooks and crannies. She spent endless hours scouring estate and garage sales, second-hand and antique stores and flea markets, too, trying to envision how each selection would fit into its new home.

She picked out several large pieces of antique wicker still in their natural state, a couple of old trunks, a set of cafe chairs and a weathered pine dining table.

She added plants and set them in wicker baskets or burnished copper pots. Table lamps were in a variety of vintage styles from brass shells to bamboo-painted pottery.

And finally she set herself the task of equipping the tiny kitchen with everything she could think of that a guest might want or need, down to a wide choice of tea and coffee flavors.

At last, when she stepped back it was with a tremendous sigh of relief. How, she proclaimed to herself, worth all the time and expense, how rewarding, though tiring, the total experience had turned out to be.

Once the exterior and interior of the house itself were completed, Helmi turned her attention to its surrounding grounds. There was much to be done in the way of soil preparation, design planning and plant selection.

For months, throughout the turbulent reconstruction period, a landscape design of broad scope had been secretly brewing in her mind. Her brain was nearly bursting with ideas. Even more than planning interiors, creating imaginative outdoor rooms was a favorite milieu.

She dubbed it the Moonlight Garden. For some reason Helmi had always felt a strong alliance with the moon. Perhaps it had something to do with its position amid the stars and planets at the time she was born. She studied it often, trying to unveil its exquisite beauty and mystery. Even its color was difficult to decipher - unlike any other light she had ever seen. In the evenings, whenever she stood staring at it, its luminescence filled her entire being with such a radiant warmth that she felt as if she were glowing all over in a golden aura.

She loved a full moon the most. Each night as it climbed up out of the trees it was as if some brilliant drama were unfolding for her alone. Somehow it seemed to be her friend, entrusting sacred secrets to her for safekeeping.

It had the face of an old soul. She drew on the hypnotic force of its power and internalized it until sometimes she felt its reflective mystery, magic, and beauty welling up within.

In order to mirror the moon's own delicate luminosity the flower colors of each plant, shrub, or tree would be in various shades of white or the palest pastels.

She envisioned a meandering path winding gently through the wooded garden. Created out of crushed beach rock, it's soft ochre color, naturally and harmoniously, would blend in with the surrounding woods.

In the vision, several unusual varieties of old favorites - magnolias, dogwoods, and an antique lilac or two - turned into focal points along the trail. Bleeding hearts, lily-of-the-valley, maidenhair ferns, lentens and sweet woodruff would be used underneath to soften the lines at ground level. They would also provide another dimension of different shapes and textures for added visual interest.

Each would have to have at least some scent, the stronger the better for Helmi, being a creature of the senses. And she considered her sense of smell to be the best developed of all.

For her, a touch of mystery was an essential ingredient in any garden. Being tucked away within its secret woodland lent it mystery enough, but she desired that unique element that would lift it to a rarefied, magical realm. Certain specimens would have to be hunted down like wild mushrooms and specially situated. She would scout out evening primroses, moon vines, and old rose climbers. Trailing jasmine to entwine the entrance arbor, flowering tobacco and wild ginger, foxgloves and columbines closer in. Certain strains of clematis could survive the leafy canopy overhead and climb among the tree trunks. The star jasmine, dogwood and magnolias would add depth and structure to the overall design.

Statuary and benches for resting, viewing or meditation would be placed at regular intervals. She even dreamed of including a pond and fountain someday. The musical sound of rushing water, she loved, as a backdrop for any garden.

Day after day she devoted to readying the soil for planting. She already had the perfect topsoil, a never-ending supply of composted horse manure, which she spread and worked lovingly into the hard root-tangled ground. She loved the working of the soil, the hoeing, raking, kneading, not unlike a gourmet chef preparing dough for the oven.

Soon she had converted the brambly thicket into a fertile clearing filled with rich, dark, fluffy bedding the color of fresh-roasted coffee beans.

Finally everything was ready to receive her variegated cache of flora which was, up to this point, little more than an extensive wish list.

From that moment on she was obsessed with tracking down the loveliest, most fragrant and delicately-hued flowers, shrubs and dwarf trees she could find to fit into her lovingly created new space.

In the days and months to come, a good deal of her time and energy was devoted to unearthing, then placing, each new-found gem.

At the Green Thumb, the bustling local nursery, she loaded up, starting with the most favored on her wish list. She could not find everything she needed and knew she would have to continue part of her search elsewhere. But she had gathered plenty of starts with which she could begin.

She could hardly wait to get back to the secret spot with her stash of greenery. And even though the selection process had been wearing, she was anxious to begin.

One by one, she carefully lowered dozens of the rarely seen trillium bulbs into their lush new home and gently covered them to just below the crown. Their fragrant, delicate white blossoms would be the first to emerge in early spring.

Next she surrounded the newly-planted bulbs with flats of sweet woodruff, a spreading herb whose white flowers are used to make May wine.

Some of the larger trees went in next as a kind of scaffolding upon which to layer the rest of the scheme. She found the perfect spot for one of a pair of star magnolias near, what would eventually be, the garden's west entrance facing the sea.

A little further along the path, she placed one of her prizes, an unusual white Chinese dogwood. Then a bit further still, making a curvilinear walkway, she set in a fragrant, blush-pink budded viburnum, a companion plant for its taller neighbor, the soft shell-pink tinted saucer magnolia.

Among the dogwoods, magnolias and viburnum, she found special spots for each of her starts of antique white lilacs. They were so fragile looking that she feared for their survival. She would have to keep close watch over them and protect them until they became fully established, which, judging from their delicacy, could be quite some time.

She stepped back, tired but pleased, to survey her handiwork. It had been a productive planting session with the bare bones of the Moonlight Garden-to-be laid into position.

The next phase would include placement of the smaller planting that would go alongside the pathway, scattered beneath and between the larger shrubs and trees.

One late summer evening she was kneeling, in her nightgown, beside the path planting woodruff when she suddenly realized she was not alone.

Startled, she looked up to see Knute standing in the gardens entrance. Wanting the finished design to be a surprise, she had been able to keep him from coming into her secret domain until this moment. This night he would not be shut out any longer. He had missed her these many months she had devoted to creating this private sanctuary. He wanted her full-fledged attention again as he had had it when they first met.

He knelt down and pulled her gently into his arms. Slowly they stood up, entwined like vines, bathed in the moonlight filtering through the branches.

As his hands ranged freely over her softness, he reveled in her nearness, the scent of her, the taste of her, the touch of her hair and skin. He had thought of this moment ever since he first saw her. It felt just as he had imagined, perfectly natural. She clung tightly to him as they lowered together to the bed of black earthy soil.

He entered her quickly, deeply, forcefully - with the sole purpose of making a reality what he had been yearning to do for so long.

She stretched and arched, like a lazy cat, upward to receive him over and over.

Getting into bed with her in the comfort and privacy of her own room was uppermost in his mind.

"Show me where your room is," he whispered, with mounting urgency, against her ear.

She led him by the hand through the arbor, along the path to the steps leading up from the garden to her room.

It was her special place where few had ever been before. It was hallowed ground where she could feel safe, comfortable and completely natural. She used it as a retreat to shut herself away from the outside world. There she found the peace and tranquility she thrived on, that nourished her inner core in the same way that the most savory gourmet meal sometimes could.

She had lovingly appointed it with fine quality fabrics and furnishings. It looked and felt of understated elegance. Everything was soft, comfortable and upholstered in all natural, yet luxurious, materials. The overall impression created a soothing backdrop for relaxation, contemplation and reflection.

Helmi had chosen an earthy palette for the pillows, bedspread, carpet and draperies. They were the colors of the things she lived with daily - sand, sea grass, sea foam. There were wicker baskets, rattan chairs and a canopied bed, each dressed in either chenille, linen or raw silk. An expanse of bronze-colored Berber wool covered the floor.

Her room symbolized, for her, a magical kingdom, a sanctuary she had rarely shared with anyone, until that moment.

As they approached the terrace steps leading up to her room, Knute saw a flood of light streaming through the French doors. Every evening, at dusk, Helmi performed her candle lighting ritual. Knute caught his breath at the sight. What he saw before him looked straight out of a fairy tale, like a tree house sitting in the midst of an enchanted forest.

He reached for Helmi and gathered her in his arms. As he gently lifted her, she instinctively grasped his neck. He carried her to her bed and laid her down as if she were the most precious of packages.

Looking around the room he beheld a lovely space that reflected the loveliness he knew dwelt within Helmi. Suddenly he felt as if he had come home, that he was where he belonged.

He stretched out beside her on the bed and pulled her to him. Seamlessly he slipped off her flimsy garments as candlelight merged with moonbeams to veil her nakedness.

In the distance, the muted sound of the sea echoed its rhythmic fugue. It provided the musical accompaniment to their lovemaking that played on well into the wee hours of the night.

In the morning, when they finally awoke, it was with awe that they surveyed the setting and each other. Sunlight filtered through the shutters, marking the carpet with zebra stripes.

"Let's have breakfast out on the terrace where we can watch the surf," Helmi whispered against Knute's ear.

"That sounds like the best idea I've heard so far today," he whispered back.

"Your job is to set up the bistro table and chairs out there while I fix our breakfast. I'll bring it up on a tray as soon as it's ready."

"Yes ma'am. Your wish is as good as granted," he answered. He was feeling completely in his element, firmly ensconced as he was, within Helmi's unique realm.

Helmi quickly wrapped herself in her cozy chenille robe to ward off the chill in the air. Then she headed into the master bath to freshen up before tackling their breakfast.

It was another of her favorite places. She thought of it as a luxury spa complete with jetted tub and thick Turkish towels. An expanse of pale ochre stone tiles covered the floor and bath surround creating a soothing retreat in which to soak, sometimes for hours, in fragrant bubbles. She lit her scented candles and wallowed in a delicious sense of well-being as her eyes floated over each detail she had tirelessly spent selecting. She especially loved the ribbed brass faucets with swan neck spouts over the two vanity sinks, both of which had a fluted design. Above each was an ornate, gold-leafed antique mirror. She remembered how excited she had been the day she found them on one of her regular antique shop forays. Matching pairs of anything antique were an extreme rarity so she had felt it to be an especially serendipitous find.

Louver doors led into the water closet alcove and covered the storage closets.

Italian stone squares enriched the vanity counter-top and back-splash in an earthy topaz color. Even the rush-mat-tinted towels enhanced the serene ambience.

Suddenly she looked up into the mirror and caught a dreamy expression on her face. She chastised herself for daydreaming and headed out to the stairway leading down to the kitchen.

Once there she was again reminded that it was one of her most favorite rooms in the entire house. It was as warm and inviting as she had originally envisioned. In recent months it had undergone an extensive facelift comprising every element on her wish list.

The center wall had been removed so that it was no longer a galley but opened up with a huge butcher-block-topped island in the middle of the room. Most of the pots, pans, and utensils were housed in it as well as shelves for her cookbook collection and an extensive assortment of wine.

The vaulted ceiling added to the heightened sense of space. But the best feature was the stone floor that made it feel like the inside of an ancient villa. The counter-tops and back-splashes were in smaller tumbled travertine tiles in the same rich ochre hue. The walls and ceiling had been troweled on with a tawny pigment mixed into the plaster to enhance the antiquated flavor.

All the upper cabinets were in a honey spice finish with mullion glass doors, including four back to back over the center island. She loved the look of all the small panes. Some, like on the main pantry doors and adjoining butler's pantry cupboards, extended floor to ceiling.

It was an ideal setting in which to be inspired to try imaginative dishes and meals. She sometimes thought how much the upgraded conditions had not only boosted her desire to cook, but elevated the quality of the food itself.

Slowly she gathered around her the necessary tools with which to prepare what she hoped would be a most delectable breakfast for Knute.

She decided on Eggs Benedict - something she hadn't tried for ages - fresh-baked croissants and fresh-squeezed orange juice, one of her favorite breakfasts for special occasions.

She pulled the croissants, made from scratch the day before, out of the bread bin along with a pat of butter. Soon the pastry was done perfectly to a rich golden brown and flaky to the touch. They always reminded her of the many gourmet meals she had savored throughout her trip to France.

Her new gas cook-top was the perfect surface on which to prepare the temperamental egg dish. While she got out the copper pan for the hollandaise sauce her mind's eye retraced time to the morning she had first ordered Eggs Benedict. She was on her honeymoon in San Francisco with her former husband. They were seated in the glass-roofed conservatory of the Sheraton Palace Hotel. The dazzling room had been converted into a palm-tree-laden dining room oasis dotted with huge pillars of sparkling white marble. The vast floor spread before her like a creamy white sea.

Overhead, sunlight streamed down through the canopy of tiny, crystal panes, illuminating the space beneath, making it glow from within.

The memory of that exquisite spot made her nostalgic, at least about the setting.

Rummaging through her silver tray collection she found an old favorite, ornately chased with handles and feet, that she had stumbled onto in a second-hand shop. Next she laid an intricately detailed antique linen napkin across its length along with her best china and silverware. Finally, she arranged a bouquet of old roses in her choicest export porcelain vase for a touch of romance.

When the coffee was ready she placed everything on the tray and carried it upstairs.

Knute was out on the terrace sprawled in one of the deck chairs beside the wrought iron dining table.

The early morning sun was just peaking up over the eastern side of the roof, warming the glass tabletop and glittering the grass in front of the terrace steps.

As soon as he spotted Helmi coming toward him, tray-laden, he was on his feet to relieve her of her heavy load.

He was instantly taken, not only with her presentation of the meal, but with the glowing vision of radiance she made.

And once again he was struck by a strange flush of heat spreading through him like a tidal wave that hit whenever she came near.

"Wouldn't you say it's time we thought about cohabiting under the same roof?" Knute needled her in his most bantering tone.

"It might eliminate quite a bit of the inconvenience we've been experiencing, over the long run," she replied, in a much steadier tone than her emotions were waging within. The idea that he had so casually just verbalized was the ever-recurring scenario she'd replayed thousands of times in her loftiest pipe-dreams.

She tried to camouflage the rising sense of euphoria she was feeling by infusing her voice with a nonchalant insouciance.

But her innards were quaking tumultuously from nervous excitement amid the angst of envisioning a myriad of changes the union might create.

Knute felt like a weather forecaster as he tried to decipher the fleeting array of moods that swept across the planes of her face.

Luckily the prevailing winds seemed to swing the tide in his favor. He watched her features soften toward the idea of sharing not only their days, nights and surrounds but, too, the moment by moment unfolding of two intensely lived lives.

She swallowed hard, gulped back her trepidations and beamed her steady gaze squarely into his mellow hazel eyes.

"How soon would you be able to move in?" she heard herself asking, as if from a long distance away.

"Would tomorrow be too late?" he asked as his mouth began to spread into a wide grin.

"I think I'll need at least a year to prepare for your arrival" *and,* she thought to herself, *for all the havoc you'll wreak once you get here.*

The next few months blurred together into a flurry of intense activity, transporting Knute's belongings from the BLM property to Wildwood.

First he had to track down a replacement, at least to occupy the living quarters. He would still keep his position but, with the advent of the additional man, would finally have a much needed assistant to help manage the land and wild herd.

It was an experienced hand named Brice Selden who answered the summons. He and Knute were extremely compatible from the first as Knute began training him in many of the duties he himself had carried out in the early days of his tenancy. He was quick to absorb the myriad of chores, duties and details that Knute flung his way and seemed game for more. The extra help eased Knute's responsibilities considerably, allowing him freedom to arrange a life more centrally revolving around Helmi and Windflower.

Their new life together consisted of hours spent locating spaces for Knute's books and arranging boxes filled with his special brand of possessions. Helmi sometimes felt as if she were learning a whole new side of the man as she, every so often, stepped back to observe him as he unpacked.

He had always been so intensely private that it gave her an opportunity to gather insight into some of his best kept secrets.

His clothes began blending seamlessly in with hers in the ample dressing room as if no drastic change had recently occurred. It was as if they, as much as Helmi and Knute, were desirous of being together.

Every item of his eventually found what seemed to be its perfect niche in the grand scheme of Helmi's world so that, little by little, a transition was evolving that allowed Knute a thoroughly natural homecoming

. . . .

PART   V

In the days and weeks that followed, Knute and Helmi worked side by side furthering along the progress they had already begun around the ranch.

Knute continued his work with Windflower to keep her muscles toned and her overall condition strong and sound.

Helmi continued developing and maintaining the various gardens she had originally designed.

During the days of their first summer together they treasured the lengthy hours of heat and slow pace in which to do chores and enjoy their leisure moments.

Every so often Helmi would surprise Knute with a picnic basket full of her homemade specialties and they would head down the trail to the beach. He would gather up some driftwood along the shore and build a roaring bonfire exactly the way Helmi loved it to be. The flames soared against a Prussian blue sea capped by white foam, setting the perfect stage for a romantic repast.

They flung down a huge, snugly throw over the warm sand and spread out the various utensils and dishes. Knute pulled out a wine opener and uncorked a special vintage Helmi had discovered hidden behind some newer labels on wooden shelving in their makeshift garage cellar.

They raised their glasses and held them suspended as Knute proposed a toast. "Here's to you, darling, who have turned every moment of my days and nights into precious nuggets of exquisite quality and beauty," he said as he clinked his glass with hers.

"That is one of the most touching tributes I have ever received from anyone," she whispered, barely able to speak so filled with emotion was she.

The weeks and months to follow were filled with a myriad

of chores, responsibilities and routine tasks needing attention but many hours of blissful times too.

Each reveled in the other's presence and seemed visibly to flourish in such a romantic environment. They spent countless hours basking in each other's company and never tired of spending time together. To each, they were precious moments, rare as jewels, to be savored and enjoyed whenever the chance arose.

One early October day Knute told Helmi that he had been called away by the BLM to assist in a major roundup of a band of wild Mustangs that needed to be culled and relocated.

"I might have to be gone as long as a month this time," he told her regretfully. By now, she expected his absences, but would never get used to them. Each time he left she seemed to miss him more than the time before but would never let on to him how much these brief separations affected her.

Instead, she put on a brave face and delved even more diligently into her chores. Caring for the animals, including Maggie, the golden retriever they had acquired soon after Knute moved in, took up a large chunk of her days. There was also a flock of black bantam hens they kept for their quality eggs and two proud peacocks with gloriously colored tail feathers.

Wild creatures of every ilk gravitated to the natural beauty of Wildwood and Helmi never turned any of them away.

But the main focus of her attention, especially when Knute went away, was always Windflower.

She would throw herself into the mare's care. The main part of her horse-keeping regimen went into grooming. For Helmi it was very therapeutic to brush and comb Windflower, to brush her coat until it shone and comb her mane and tail until they glistened.

She loved to see the copper in her tri-colored coat gleam like a new penny after she had been wet down, scrubbed, shampooed and towel dried. That was when her markings all vied with each other for attention and her Appaloosa characteristics were most distinctive. That was when Windflower looked her most distinguished. Even her hooves were polished so that their unique striations stood out against the ground.

She seemed to sense she looked her best and stood tall and erect, then pranced proudly around the pasture before she knelt down to take her first post-bath roll in the dirt. But even the prodigious amount of sand couldn't mar her exquisite coloration or conformation and she remained as lovely as ever.

Late one October evening, when Knute had been gone with the BLM for about a week, Helmi awoke suddenly and immediately sensed something strange in the air.

She threw on the robe laying across the foot of her bed, ran to the window and looked out, beyond the southern boundary of her property.

The night sky, usually so deep, dark, and mysterious was lit up and glowing the color of burnished coal embers. The silhouetted landscape stood out against the luminous tangerine backdrop as brightly visible as though it were dawn. But glancing back at the bedside clock she saw that it was only a little after two.

She felt her stomach start to churn and her heart begin to race as fear and panic slowly set in. But before they could get too strong a grip on her, she made a Herculean effort to calm herself so she could decide what to do next.

When she had gathered enough nerve to look outside again, the once pastoral vista was a blazing wall of flames flickering in the distance.

Moving in time with some silent musical accompaniment it danced and swayed as lyrically as if it had been choreographed for some classical ballet.

The golden glow was intensifying and the curtain-like expanse of flames was gathering momentum, all the while advancing along the horizon. Nothing was visible but the raging blood orange background voraciously devouring everything in its path and moving nearer with each passing moment, consuming everything in its destructive wake.

Temporarily mesmerized by the hypnotic mass, heaving and swaying like a massive dragon, she shook her head and suddenly snapped into action.

Her palms had broken into a sweat and her fingers trembled as she snatched up the phone and dialed 911.

Vaguely, she recalled later, the operator asking her, "What do you see?"

"It looks like a wall of fire is moving this way. It's getting closer and it's coming fast. Please tell them to hurry. My barn is in its path."

She remembered, too, giving directions to get to her property and how to find her approach road.

Then the unfathomable happened. It was a sound she would never forget for all the rest of her days. Hysterical screaming was coming from the barn. Shrill, terrified screams rang through the stark blackness, causing goose bumps to make her skin crawl.

Windflower was calling to her. Cry after cry echoed through the night as Helmi raced out to help her.

Visions of a thousand idyllic days during Windflower's life flashed in front of her as she ran out to her.

When she finally reached the barn after what seemed an eternity, what she saw would scar her memory like a hideous gash.

Windflower's beautiful head and face were virtually unrecognizable. Starting from her forehead the skin was hanging loose. Everywhere, other than the two holes for her eyes, was either charred or completely gone.

One whole side of her body was shriveled from the intense heat of the flames. The normally thick pad of fur was gone and in its place was a huge, raw, gaping wound oozing bubbling yellowish slime.

Helmi had never felt such a sickness at the pit of her stomach and it took all the will power she could muster not to fall down in a dead faint.

Sobs wracked her to the depths of her core as she ran to the tack room to grab the lead rope.

Somewhere in the background she heard the dirge of the sirens as the fire trucks began to arrive and hoses pulled in every direction.

When she got back to the barn, the firemen had doused the worst of the flames so that only a veil-like smokescreen remained and blurred the interior.

She had never heard the sounds emanating from Windflower who had shrunk back into the blackness of the stall as if knowing how horribly disfigured she had become.

They were soft, mewing moans amid heavier gurgling gasps as if she were a drowning swimmer fighting for air.

Slowly Helmi approached the shivering, panicked mare and, finding a small path around her neck that hadn't been scorched, gently slid the lead rope up, over and around it, carefully trying not to rub the massively wounded area.

Too traumatized to resist, Windflower put up little fight as Helmi urged her forward, with familiar whispered signals, out of the barn gate and across the roadway to the pasture.

Somehow she managed to find an intact, dry flake of soft hay and spread it out flat over a large space. Then she encouraged Windflower to lay down on the side free from injury before she ran back to the house to call the mare's vet's emergency number.

He was there within an hour with salve, gauze, penicillin, Bute tablets for the pain and a light summer sheet to keep dirt from causing infection.

The possibility of her going into shock was another major cause of his concern. The sheet was slightly insulated as well as ventilated with perforated holes to allow the wound to breathe.

After the vet had gone, Helmi curled up beside the mare and never once left her side throughout the rest of the night.

The sight she saw, when she awoke from a fitful sleep, etched an indelible impression in her memory. Most of the barn was gone, a charred mass of smoldering timbers. Only one of the stalls would be habitable to house Windflower. The rest was a rubble heap of debris.

Windflower lay on her side wrapped in gauze and a sheet of netting, looking like a mummy. Steady groaning, accompanied by each raspy breath, created a sound in the background like a muffled fugue.

Dr. Shelton, the attending veterinarian, had given Helmi detailed instructions about dressing Windflower's wounds with salve and fresh gauze. He warned her it would be a long, slow healing process and they would be constantly battling the threat of infection. But Helmi instinctively knew her two worst enemies would be, not infection, but discouragement and depression.

All she could think of doing during the hours and days ahead was to gently cushion Windflower in her arms and hum familiar tunes in her ear in a feeble attempt to comfort her.

She was obviously in excruciating pain, her wounds were oozing thick yellow pus and the sounds emanating from her were unrecognizable to Helmi. She could only remain the helpless observer, silently willing some magical healing powers to materialize.

In the interim moments when she wasn't tending Windflower, she immersed herself in researching natural and traditional curative methods used in the treatment of severe burns.

She spent hours at the local library nearby pouring over prodigious amounts of documentation and case histories, though they invariably pertained to humans rather than animals.

She was particularly fascinated by the studies involving the usage of medicinal herbs dating back centuries.

During much intensive investigation, one coincidence in particular intrigued her. It had to do with the fact that the Northwest Coast Native Americans routinely used herbs for healing a myriad of ailments and which were very prominent in their daily lives.

She began rifling through reams of volumes pertaining to Native American herbal remedies. Simultaneously she studied formulas they used in the creation of poultices for serious burns, jotting them down on a stack of recipe cards.

One day she was with Windflower in the pasture, holding her head on her lap, when suddenly she felt tightly squeezed from behind.

"I got your message and hustled home as fast as I could," Knute whispered in her ear.

"I thought you'd never get here," she sighed in relief as she leaned back and snuggled against him.

"How bad is she?" he asked and she could hear the dread in his low tone of voice.

"Take a good look for yourself," she entreated him. "The vet said her wounds will get a lot worse before they, and she, begin to get any better. We all have a long, slow road ahead to climb together if she's to have any kind of quality of life again."

She watched as Knute gently took hold of Windflower's head and placed it on his lap, the tears streaming down his face.

"My poor, poor, precious Windflower," he cooed softly in her ear. "You're going to be all right. We're going to heal you. We're going to will you to be well. With your spirit and stubbornness and our tenacity, you're going to be good as new."

Helmi could only watch in awe as the two most important beings in her life swayed together, one softly moaning in agony while the other, his teeth gritted in steely determination, vowed to heal her.

One by one a steady caravan of sleepless nights and endless days ministering moral support to Windflower while doctoring her near-fatal wounds, led Knute and Helmi down the long, slow road to recovery.

One day Helmi came to Knute with what came to be known as one of her "ingenious brainstorms".

"Why don't we turn at least half of the garage into a kind of experimental laboratory. There's a lot of extra space that's going to waste when we could be using it to create a concoction that might help Windflower to heal," she began, mapping out the initial steps necessary in order to begin turning out Windflower's medicinal brew. "We could set up a production line of pots in which our herbal ingredients could steep and simmer."

Knute listened intently, astounded as usual, by Helmi's vaulting imagination which, as usual, left him trailing behind.

But he also could see the logic behind her reasoning and knew they not only had nothing to lose by attempting it, but possibly much to achieve.

"After we set up the assembly line, what would be the next step?" Knute prodded her to further develop her theory.

"Well, we'd have to begin by harvesting literally tons of the key ingredient - the seaweed. It would have to be brought up from the beach and stacked into what would become huge composting piles where it would begin breaking down into manageable clumps," she continued unfolding her plan, pleased and encouraged by his obvious enthusiasm and interest.

Knute could virtually track the progress of her mental wheels hurtling along, gathering momentum as the tiny seedpod of invention broke into being.

"I learned from my recent research that, besides the seaweed, other key ingredients are also necessary to mix with it in order to create the healing properties forming the poultice," she explained.

"What would the rest of the salve consist of?" Knute asked, visibly intrigued by the mysterious process Helmi was so patiently describing.

"The other main ingredients would be Vitamin B-12 plus a nutrient-rich cocktail of cod liver oil, sesame oil, calcium, iron, potassium, and a puree of sage leaves and avocado," she explained. "Just about every other trace mineral would also be combined with the other elements. And finally cooked salal leaves would be woven into a kind of bandage to form the outer protective membrane for the top dressing. From what I've read, everything would have to be cooked very slowly for a long time over low heat. It's an age-old fermentation process, a critical factor for the end result to be effective," she concluded.

"Let's get started, the sooner the better for Windflower's sake," Knute effused. "Tomorrow we can start gathering up the seaweed. There's bound to be mountains of it laying around since this last storm we've had over the past few days. We can take the tractor-trailer down to the beach and load up. I'll throw it onto compost piles while you set up the makeshift laboratory," he added.

I'll go out this afternoon and get the necessary supplies and utensils," she offered. "It's a good thing we've already got the old stove set up out there. We can use that for brewing the potion. The list is a long one, but I'm pretty sure I'll be able to find everything we're going to need."

And so began their journey into homeopathic medicine engendered by the deep need of their grievously injured, beloved Windflower.

Within days everything was set up to begin production. Helmi had the makeshift laboratory kitchen transformed into an efficient assembly line. Every ingredient was in place to be poured, scraped or chopped into the huge main kettle. Great bunches of seaweed were stored nearby in the spare refrigerator, after being brought in from Knute's carefully orchestrated compost bins.

From then on, they spent every waking moment experimenting with cooking times, temperatures, textures and amounts. They discovered it took endless hours to reach just the right thickness. Gradually it was possible for them to tell when the mixture had reached its final phase by its color and consistency.

Finally they had a sufficiently aged amount to begin the application to a small area of Windflower's massive wound.

They decided to use finely meshed gauze pads on which they spread the poultice mix. Then with the slightest possible touch, each in turn softly pressed the pad against the charred horseflesh until Windflower shrieked for them to stop. At first her cry came after only seconds but with each passing day, the amount of time spent pressing the soothing balm onto the ragged skin lasted longer and longer. Windflower was becoming calmer with every new application and eventually even acted as if she were expecting some feeling of relief.

The process was extremely time-consuming because of the vastly affected area. But, little by little, every square inch was treated with the precious balm and with the most tender loving care by both Helmi and Knute until, miraculously, they began to see the slightest hints of visible results.

They noticed the yellow pus dissipating along with the blackened blisters. And the swelling and redness, too, were slowly receding.

It was a painfully labor-intensive period for Knute and Helmi. Thus far they had invested hundreds of hours of devoted care toward Windflower's rehabilitation with their intricately sensitive experiment.

But the long months of selfless ministrations to one willful, bullheaded mare with the gypsy spirit seemed to be gradually paying off.

Miraculously her hideous wounds were, daily, showing slight hints of improvement. At first, in those early days, they didn't have much to cling to or encourage them to believe that they were on the right track.

Until, slowly, small signs of hope shone forth. Windflower seeming hungry, Windflower acting thirsty, Windflower getting on her feet. Then, Windflower trying to eat, Windflower starting to drink, Windflower managing to take a few steps. Slow, small signs though they were, they were slow, small but steady, steps of progress.

After many long, grueling, often frustrating, months of rehabilitation those varied signs were incredibly heartening and so welcome to Helmi and Knute. They felt immense gratification, wholeheartedly embracing the fruitful rewards of their Herculean efforts.

And, gradually, they became aware of something else through those long, sleepless months of ministering potions, brews and poultices as well as selfless devotion. They realized not only the astounding curative potential of seaweed, but, more surprising, the remarkable recuperative powers that Windflower possessed to an almost miraculous degree.

They had witnessed her impressive comeback from the serious leg injury she had sustained, what seemed like, ages ago. So they had an inkling of something in her inner trove of special abilities.

But her intrepid transition from near-fatal wounds toward full recovery was more like a living testament to her extraordinary healing powers.

....

PART VI

With Windflower well on the road to full recovery, Knute and Helmi felt freed up to rekindle their sadly neglected relationship.

Knute, keenly sensitive to Helmi's every mood and desire, knew instinctively that she yearned for an old-fashioned courtship, THE Grand Passion, that neither time nor circumstances had bestowed. Deep in his soul it was what he, too, desired from the moment they'd laid eyes on each other. He also knew that he had it within him to be the romantic prince of her fairy-tale dreams.

One time she even confessed to him, how, ever since she was a little girl, she had dreamt of a princely suitor who passionately pursued her. And, in her fantasy, she was wooed in the most exquisitely romantic manner, that unfolded very poetically and beautifully. Every detail she described about her imaginary amour was glittering and dazzling, like a magical, enchanted kingdom.

It was a great deal for Knute to absorb and an even greater amount for him to fulfill.

But the more he thought about bringing all of her wishes to fruition, the more he felt up to the challenge and ready to embark on his amatory adventure.

He began to map out an elaborate strategy in his own mind and, in the process, let his imagination flow more freely than it ever had. Conjuring up alluring ways to seduce Helmi turned into a complex game of chance.

One arena that was especially familiar to both of them was

the kitchen. The myriad intimate evenings spent lingering over elaborately prepared dishes, had, each time, bound them more closely together. He vowed to focus much of his attention designing delicious dinners to delight her. Up until then Helmi had planned and prepared most of their meals. So Knute decided to step in and turn their usual way of doing things upside down.

He set his sights on haute cuisine and began poring through numerous gourmet cookbooks.

Whenever he had a stretch of time to spare, he snuck out to used book stands and cookbook sales in search of gourmet treats. In the process he ended up scanning hundreds of delectable menu ideas.

He was determined to dazzle her with his cooking prowess by creating artistic, imaginative dining experiences. Each Herculean effort he made would be one more unique way of showing his love for her. He would woo her with food.

Helmi had taught him reams in the decorative department which he drew on to come to his aid.

Every Saturday evening he began his courting ritual by laying an exquisitely appointed dining table using an antique lace cloth. Next came the beeswax candles for the ornate brass candelabras. Candlelight was the one essential element they had grown accustomed to and could not exist without. Simple tasks, such as polishing old sterling silver pieces, provided him the opportunity to muse on the coming evening. Images of intimate moments reverberated through his imagination.

Lovingly he lavished each setting with elegant bone china, cut crystal and old linen.

Lastly he chose the Chinese vase, filled it with Oriental lilies and other flowers and tenderly placed it in the middle of it all as the exquisite centerpiece.

The ritualistic performance of each intricate set of details became part of the fabric of his romantic pursuit.

Knute's passionate wooing, pursuing, and ultimately marrying Helmi had begun in earnest......

With each passing day, their fairy-tale continued to unfold. And with each passing day she fell more passionately in love with Knute. He was her sun and her moon, her stars and her sky. Her whole world orbited around him, the centerpiece that sent her entire universe reeling wildly on its axis. And he never failed to stir a sense of excitement in her whenever he drew near.

She secretly spied on his sumptuous cuisine preparations with dual emotions of awe and disbelief.

The dramatically unfolding scenario, like good theatre, was both delightfully surprising and deliciously sensual. That he would go to such elaborate lengths just to please her, filled her with wonder - to be his muse was, for her, a truly moving revelation. The resulting outcome was that he endeared himself to her more inextricably than ever before.

One of the evenings he intended to be light-years more intimately romantic than any he had previously created. It was to be the culmination of his intricately designed courting tapestry, interwoven with part wooing, part pursuing, all bound together with a golden filigree of love.

The setting he selected for such a momentous occasion was the diminutive conservatory leading directly off of the dining room. Completely enclosed on three sides with tiny-paned windows and double French doors leading to the garden, it lent, for Knute, the perfect note of intimacy.

That night was to be the apogee of all their evenings and, tucked within it, that magical moment, the much anticipated marriage proposal. Every detail, every nuance, every bit of ambiance had to be exquisite.

He sifted through the recipes he'd designated as reserved for special occasions and came across a scrumptious-looking picture of Herb Roasted Chicken. Its skin was a buttery golden brown, sprinkled with minced Italian parsley and bits of chopped French tarragon. To compliment the chicken he would prepare oven roasted new potatoes, fresh spring peas with pearl onions and coconut cream pie for dessert.

Their evening would begin with cocktails and hors d'oeuvres in front of the living room fireplace. Helmi loved to sit in front of a roaring fire every night. She had also schooled Knute in the fine art of mixing Russian vodka martinis, of which he now considered himself somewhat of a connoisseur.

He knew two of Helmi's favorite delicacies were a soft St. Andre cheese spread on a mini Tuscan loaf. So he would serve ample amounts of both. After cocktails they would proceed to the conservatory for his lovingly prepared dinner.

Something special was in the air, Helmi suspected, with her well-honed sixth sense. Knute, too, had hinted that it wasn't going to be one of their usual evenings and that she should fantasize freely while choosing her outfit and dressing.

Meanwhile he was dressing the table with the ornate, cut-linen cloth and matching napkins, silver candlesticks, sterling silverware, and crystal champagne flutes. It was going to be a very sumptuous affair.

He brought in some more fresh-cut roses and lilies-of-the-valley to add to the lovely Oriental vase he had already placed in the center of the tiny table. Next he found a silver ice bucket for the champagne and placed a bottle of Veuve Cliquot in the refrigerator to chill.

The chicken was thickly basted with sweet cream butter, dressed with salt, pepper, and the freshly cut herbs and placed in the oven to slow roast. Then he rushed upstairs to shower and change for the evening's festivities.

Helmi kept secreted away from Knute in the guest bedroom so he wouldn't be able to see her until she came downstairs. She had set aside a brand new evening dress and saved it to wear for just such an occasion.

Knute donned the tuxedo he'd never worn. He was already downstairs when   Helmi descended the stairs. She looked, to Knute, like a golden goddess. He had never seen her look so lovely. She was shimmering, all golden and glowing. Her gown was incandescent and glittered as if sprinkled with flecks of gold leaf.

But nothing could match the radiance she exuded, like a candle lit from within. He could not take his eyes off her classically elegant beauty. She epitomized the vision in his recurring dream he referred secretly to as the Dream of Gold, that he had dreamt so many nights while sleeping. She was the manifestation of Woman incarnate, the one he had always envisioned loving.

Moments before Helmi made her dramatic entrance, Knute lit the fire and all the candles in the house were aglow. To Helmi, everything seemed infused with a soft golden sheen, lending all she saw an exquisite luminosity.

She fought to catch her breath as Knute, exuding his own dark, brooding brand of magnetism, rose to greet her. He was, in his tuxedo, looking his most dashing.

"You look ravishing," he gasped as she glided over to greet him with a kiss on the cheek. "May I fix you something to drink?" he asked.

"That's an excellent idea. I'll have a vodka martini straight up, please," she responded, all the while held firmly in place by his eyes, as they slowly disrobed her.

"I'll have the same since that is now my specialty and the best possible choice," he said.

"They are delectable alright. It's too bad they're so addictive. I could drink that whole shaker full of them," she admitted.

"Please be seated while I make those and bring in the hors d'oeuvres," he said, gesturing toward the loveseat near the fire.

He then disappeared into the kitchen where sounds of clattering plates, cupboards, and slamming refrigerator doors were heard in the background.

Soon he emerged with an elegant silver tray filled with delicacies. He held it out for her to sample one.

"This is delicious," she effused, her voice muffled as she bit into the bread. "What kind of cheese is it?"

"Your favorite French, St. Andre, on a fresh loaf of Tuscan," he called over his shoulder as he disappeared into the wet bar to mix the martinis.

Her glass, she noticed when it arrived, was chilled to perfection. One plump garlic-stuffed olive sat in the center of the vodka. Sipping slowly, she thought she had never tasted anything more delicious. He definitely seemed to possess the magic formula for making a world-class martini. *Or is it,* she mused, *because I find him so appetizing that I find everything he does equally delicious?*

Finally he took his chair near her in front of the fire and raised his glass for the toast.

"To the alluring Helmi, the one woman I desire above all others and want at my side for the rest of my life. And, to eternal love," he said softly, touching his glass to hers, gentle as a caress.

"To eternal love and to you, darling," she whispered as she

returned the caress by pressing her glass to his, visibly moved by the gravity of the moment.

While Helmi slowly sipped her drink, she reveled in the time it allowed to survey the mysterious creature across from her. He was still a monumental enigma to her, even after all the time they had spent together. She knew she could never tire of him. He was too complex for that. He was like a vintage antique, only improving with age.

Those were some of the sentiments racing through her mind as he led her, by the hand, into the candlelit conservatory for what he hoped would be a festive engagement celebration.

Helmi was spellbound by the beauty of the setting, and by the care and thought that had gone into every exquisite detail. He had managed to find, among her treasures, not only the best pieces, but her favorites, too.

The elegant cutwork linen tablecloth glimmered luminously in the candlelight that gilded the silver, china, crystal and flowers in a soft, golden haze. The scent of tea and jasmine emanated from the bouquet of roses, lilies-of-the-valley and Oriental lilies, suffusing the room with an intoxicating perfume.

The entire scene was the culmination of a romantic Knute she had never seen to quite such an extent. She had known occasional romantic moments with him before but never with such an intense sense of purpose.

Suddenly she realized he had set the stage for something truly momentous, and embraced the idea with her whole heart. That night, she imagined, was going to be the highlight of all their times together.

She was enchanted, floating in a magical fantasy dreamscape. It was as if she were peering through golden-hued lenses. Everything before her was incandescent, her golden childhood fairy-tale coming to fruition.

The innermost secret chamber of her soul exulted in imagining the climactic moment of his proposal. The idea of actually being married to him she had rarely entertained. But suddenly as it moved into the realm of possibility, euphoria coursed through her body and lit it up like lightning striking.

He held out her chair for her to be seated, then headed back out to the kitchen to add some final flourishes.

First he brought in their salads served on her ornate gold-rimmed china. The crisp romaine lettuce was laced with avocado, tossed with a tangy Italian vinaigrette and elegantly garnished with anchovies. Helmi savored the quality and freshness of each special ingredient and reveled in the delicacy of flavors. He had used the best lettuce and only the choicest olive oil.

When they had finished, he whisked their dishes away with the efficiency of the most seasoned waiter.

Next he set up the stand and silver champagne bucket filled with ice and brought in the chilled Veuve Cliquot which he lovingly nestled in among the shavings. The champagne flutes were superb creations, finely ribbed, hand-blown crystal set above a bulbous gold-specked midriff.

With great panache, he wrapped the precious bottle in a white cloth, unwound the protective wiring and ejected the cork, making a loud, festive pop.

The luminous amber elixir created a dazzling display in the glasses, its glittery effervescence backlit by the candle flame.

They held up their glasses for the toast. As the ambrosial liquid slipped down her throat, Helmi thought it had the taste of an exquisitely rare vintage.

It was a divinely poised moment as well. She felt her entire future hanging by a slender thread as the evening's drama unfolded.

She watched Knute, in slow motion, reach into his pocket and pull out a tiny gold box.

It glimmered magically in the candlelight, sweeping her up in the hypnotic grip of its powerfully magnetic spell.

Slowly, like some gift-bearing genie, he opened the lid and moved in closer for her inspection. Her amazed gasp, exactly the reaction he had hoped to elicit, caused him to smile.

It was the most exquisite engagement ring she had ever beheld, as if she had selected it herself.

Seven rows of tiny pavé diamonds were set into a band of gold with a narrow rim of gold encasing them on each side. The center of the diamonds was raised in a gently curving dome to add to its allure.

Knute slowly began to slip it on her finger as he solemnly intoned the age-old words, "Will you do me the honor of becoming my wife?"

And when she raised her eyes to his, she saw they were suffused with the most loving expression she had ever seen. His radiant face exuded pure love.

"To be your wife would truly be a great honor," she answered his sentiment like an echo, "but also the greatest blessing ever bestowed on me."

She could not keep from staring at the dazzling ring on her finger, sparkling magically in the candle glow. It was as if it had been designed especially for her. It looked and felt elegant and fit perfectly. She sensed instinctively it would always be one of her most prized possessions.

Knute heaved a huge sigh of relief as he refilled their flutes in celebration of their newly engaged status. It was finally official after what had been an extraordinarily intense period of adjustment.

"You are the only man I have ever loved," she confessed, as she touched her glass to his, "or ever could love."

He was too touched to speak, but knew deep within his soul that he loved her in exactly the same way.

Before she detected any tears welling up in his eyes, he rushed out of the room, mumbling over his shoulder that the chicken was ready to be served.

A bit of an anticlimax, she smiled to herself, *after such an exquisite prelude.* Yet, inside, she had never before felt such bliss as flooded through her body at that moment.

All of a sudden Knute pushed open the French doors and, with great aplomb, strode in laden with a silver platter bearing buttery herb-roasted chicken and vegetables.

The aromas mingling with that of the herb-roasted potatoes and baby carrots were intoxicating, making Helmi swoon dizzily.

With a great flourish he set the tray on the side buffet and transferred servings of chicken pieces and vegetables to the elegantly trimmed dinner plates.

As Helmi slowly savored each mouthful, the flavors merged on her palate delectably.

At last Knute put away his waiter's garb and joined her for the chicken entrée. It turned out to be superbly prepared, tender, juicy, and browned to golden perfection.

Up to that moment, the entire meal was a gourmand's delight, totally rich and filling. And it was a newly-engaged woman's dream to be so attentively tended by her brand new fiancé.

Just when it seemed that dinner had come to a scintillating finale, Knute stood and, once more, began clearing dishes off the table and buffet. He was too excited by the evening's festivities to be still for long. His adrenalin was flowing simply from watching Helmi revel in the whole heady experience of being the beautiful heroine for one magical evening.

"Now what are you up to?" she asked, her curiosity genuinely piqued.

"Try to contain your excitement." he teased, while he was gathering up the tray full of dishes. As he left the room he coyly added, "It's the long awaited moment of the evening, the Grand Finale - dessert."

"Am I entitled to know what it is, or is it a tightly guarded secret?" she lightly prodded.

"It's one you always say you would love to serve but seemed neither to have the time nor the inclination to fix. So I'm preparing it especially for you in honor of this auspicious occasion," he offered as a tidbit to feed her voracious curiosity.

"It's a tremendous amount of work but you're absolutely worth all the extra effort, in my book," he assured her.

"If it's coconut cream pie, I'm utterly flabbergasted," she confessed.

"You're warm, you're very, very warm. In fact, you're hot. You've guessed it. And now you're about to taste it," he said, enjoying their little game of intrigue.

"Don't tell me you really are fixing coconut cream pie," she said incredulously.

"The one and only," he nodded yes, preening like a proud peacock, pleased by her obvious delight.

And so the dessert course began, with Knute wheeling in the serving trolley piled with gilded plates and luscious looking pie. He laid her piece in front of her. Such pie the likes of which she had never ever seen.

It was thickly topped with stiff peaks of whipped cream gently covering a rich layer of buttery custard, then sprinkled with fluffy flakes of coconut. Each delicious bite was a fittingly magical ending of the magical meal of a truly magical evening.

To the end of her days, Helmi knew she would always hold dear to her heart the memory of that one gilded night. It was all so dazzling and golden, so glowing and glamorous. But best of all it was, up to that moment in her life, the most romantic time she had ever known. She wanted to preserve it by permanently etching it upon her heart forever.

Knute's Dream of Gold had soon become a shared vision that the two worked tirelessly to bring to fruition. He very patiently described to Helmi, in vivid detail, how each intricate facet was an integral element of an exquisite whole.

She was enraptured by the scope of his visionary grand design for their future. It was an elaborate road-map with many fascinating ports of call along the way. They were all magical places she could not fathom missing. In fact, she did not want to miss a single moment of such an ambitiously adventurous master plan. She was drawn into its vortex as into the eye of some centrifugal force. And he understood instinctively that her essence comprised the lifeblood of its central core.

The next key stop along their journey would be the fairy-tale wedding. And so an extended period of planning and preparations ensued. It became like a strategically orchestrated march up to the day on which the elegant affair would finally unfold.

One of their most important decisions was where the ceremony and reception following were to be held.

It was instantaneously unanimous. They would host the event right at their own beloved Wildwood Ranch. Everything they could possibly need was right there - the lush and picturesque setting, acreage for a dozen rows of outdoor seating and even a rose-covered arbor under which the nuptials would take place.

Mostly it would entail a masterful feat of organization. The grounds would need a huge amount of attention in order to appear appropriately groomed. The reception would require tending to a myriad amount of detail. Then there were the invitations to select and send out, but not before the guest list had been compiled. They would need to choose the music as well as the musicians to sing and perform it.

And, the last part, still to come, would be the best, planning the honeymoon from a blended list of each of their most coveted romantic spots to visit.

They began by divvying up the hefty amount of responsibilities. Knute was designated to be in charge of the grounds' maintenance. Helmi elected to oversee the reception details in addition to designing the décor for the entire outdoor wedding production. It was going to be a glorious day, but it was a date that had yet to be set.

Knute immediately pitched in to tackle the massive pruning operation. Most of Helmi's gardens were enclosed by boxwood hedging that constantly needed trimming. Skillful with the hedge pruning shears, he methodically wended his way along each hedge enclosure until each one was neatly clipped. The dramatically improved appearance brought him immense gratification, spurring him on to ever greater feats.

Vast amounts of lawn covered the lush acreage needing vast amounts of weeding, watering, and fertilizing. So he devised a taxing schedule of tender loving care for keeping the extensive grounds green and manicured. Using his characteristic modus operandi of product experimentation, trial, error, and practice, he began to see gratifying results and, little by little, had the entire place looking its very best.

Setting up a master plan for managing the property, he alternated his duties among a variety of chores. The hedge trimming was in much less frequent need than the lawn regimen, which was a constantly ongoing process, a work in progress.

There were the flower beds to mulch with his own nutrient-rich compost and then apply the even richer top dressing. The plantings were set off in strong contrast against the luscious black background. The sweet fragrance of the soil always reminded him of the morning coffee ritual and aromas as he ground and brewed the exotic beans of the same dark, rich hue as the earth.

Some days he would take time out, take a step back to survey his handiwork and try objectively to determine any inroads he might have made. Some days fared better than others. Those were the times he felt genuinely rewarded for his efforts, to stare out onto the park-like setting surrounding him and see an oasis of peace and tranquility. On such days as those he thought of Wildwood Ranch as his own little slice of paradise.

On one such day in particular he was gazing pensively over the land before him and far out into the distance. His eyes scanned the backdrop of majestic trees. He sensed something about the sentinel-like row of shore pines hovering over all the others. There was a hauntingly lyrical quality about them. Reflecting back on the war he had been waging with the half-wilderness Helmi was hoping he would be able to tame, he mused to himself:

> *No amount of back-breaking toil of mine is going to check the exuberance of this landscape. This is sheer wild beauty in it purest form. done to contain its wild nature will ever tame it. It is undiluted beauty at its most romantic. These wildly swaying pines, hemlocks, and firs will go on swaying wildly long after I am gone. These tall grasses will go undulating wildly on long into perpetuity. And this sea of native plants and shrubs will look exactly the same,encased in all its beautiful wilderness,a thousand years from now, no matter what is done to alter it. Such unadulterated beauty is indelibly etched upon my mind, as it is now untarnished eternally. We will go on battling it back, wrestling it into a semblance of what we envision we want it to be. We will continue clipping and pruning and digging and chopping. But the essence of the wild beauty of this exquisite natural setting will be forever triumphant.*

The woods, the gardens, the wilderness were as a haunting fugue-like echo of the wild beauty he found by the sea that ultimately seeped into every crevice of his soul.....

After paying such an emotional tribute to wild beauty it took a long while for Knute to be able to refocus his attention onto the daunting challenge that lay ahead.

It was already almost the middle of March. They had finally chosen the wedding date. It would be in August, when the gardens were putting on their peak performance. They always bloomed unseasonably late compared to other places. Most of the year, the weather was relatively mild but, usually in August, it heated up considerably which the plants loved and flourished in such rare warmth.

So they continued the countdown, day by day, crossing off of their lengthy priority list every exquisite detail as each came into reality from being merely a pipe-dream.

Knute began constructing the arbor where they would take their vows. They selected the site for it to be at the entrance to the Rose Garden. That special spot held great significance for Helmi since the Rose Garden had become her favorite of all the gardens at Wildwood. The panoramic view from the arbor spanned the pinwheel design layout. Each of the pie-shaped wedges was edged in box and planted with old rose bushes and French lavender. An Italianate-style bubbling fountain served as the central focal point and became the heart of the garden.

Roses were Helmi's passion. She had lovingly chosen the dozens of varieties from various sources. Her collection was in a constant state of flux, ever expanding and changing. She loved the old roses best, the ones bred sometime before 1867. Even though they were often more difficult to track down, the hunt played a large part in some of her most exciting finds.

She had to admit that romantic names also often influenced her choices. Mysterious names like Mme. Sombreuil, Mme. Isaac Pereire, Gloire de Dijon, and Mme. Jules Gravereaux were a constant source of wonder. Who were the originals? And why were they so honored?

The arbor added one more element of charm to the already charming setting. It provided just the perfect romantic dimension to their future wedding site that Knute and Helmi delighted in.

Helmi watched patiently as Knute wrassled with the myriad pieces to the structure. It was going to be gorgeous, she was sure. Made of rough hewn cedar, it was double-wide with a gracefully arching top. The sides were narrow strips of lath placed in a square lattice pattern.

Several days later it was finally assembled and installed in its proper place. Helmi immediately began envisioning it lushly smothered in heavily perfumed, climbing, old roses. She imagined both sides covered, one side with one of her most favorite, the old French charmer, Gloire de Dijon, the other side with Alchymist. She would place the order with a nursery she knew specializing in old garden roses and could hardly wait to get them and put them in the ground. They would either still be blooming, she supposed, or re-blooming well into August.

To add to the garden's comfort and charm she placed an English-style teakwood, loveseat-size bench at the far end of the garden to get the best vista of the fountain and overview of much of the rest of the property, even a miniscule slice of the sea.

By the time he finished the arbor, it was again time to weed, water, and mulch all of the flower beds. Never-ending amounts of chores on his to do list were a daily struggle to stay on top of. Luckily he had a well-honed, well-rehearsed regimen with many ingenious time-saving shortcuts.

Helmi, too, had a prodigious amount to attend to before the designated August day arrived. She wanted to find just the right invitations. She was searching for an elegantly engraved script on high quality, card-stock, creamy-colored paper.

She finally found exactly what she was looking for in a very exclusive catalogue she received from the Cartier jewelry company, which just happened to create wedding invitations as well. The first step, after ordering at least four dozen to be printed up, was to prepare the guest list, including many distant friends and relatives with whom she had lost touch long ago. The wedding should be, she truly believed, an excellent reason for reconnecting.

Over the next several weeks, she drew up sketches of floral bouquets, decorative garlands for the tables and her bridal bouquet. From there she moved on to planning the menu for the reception dinner, including champagne, to be catered by a local chef.

She determined to create the most romantic bouquets possible using her beloved pale roses, creamy peonies, Casablanca lilies, blush-colored Oriental lilies, and jasmine blossoms. The exotically perfumed fragrance would be powerfully delicious. And there would be thousands and thousands of apricot blush petals in tiny golden nets for the guests to toss in the air at them.

Still yet to get were her wedding gown, head piece, and matching shoes.

Since just a little girl, she had been a passionate daydreamer. Ensconced in her room with her fairy book stories, she envisioned herself floating down the aisle shrouded in something frothy and golden. It would swirl around her, billowy like a gilded cloud and be ornately overlaid with a rich, filmy, filigreed scroll pattern. Its inspiration would be borrowed from an Old World style of design with a very European look. The quality would be superb and of the very finest workmanship.

So, at that moment in time, to find that very fairy-tale dress became her number one, first priority. She put everything else on hold, temporarily, to concentrate all of her energy on finding the golden gown of her dreams.

Leaving Knute to continue taming the wilderness that was ever encroaching onto their property, she set out on her treasure hunt, searching for a stash of wedding booty.

She immediately headed for Aurora, the nearest shopping Mecca for their area. Once there it took her some time to acclimate herself to the hustle and bustle scurrying around her. She so rarely traveled any long distance from home, that when she did venture into the city, it rapidly became completely overwhelming.

Feeling a bit dizzy and slightly disoriented, she headed toward the Topaz District, as it was called, where most of the high end boutiques were located. It was a kind of lush gardenlike oasis in the midst of the main commercial hub.

Soon she came upon a very tiny shop lushly clad in ivy and sporting a chic black-painted door. It had a beautiful, hand-lettered sign with the French name, La Belle Vie, printed in an elaborate script.

Inside was a dazzling array of bridal gowns of every shape and style all in romantic pastel shades, lining every wall. It reminded her of a Degas pastel of a dance studio stuffed with ballet costumes just waiting for the dancers to step into. She felt as if she were in a bride's heaven, everything looked so lovely.

She began working her way around the room, pulling out one dress after another, studying the style, feeling the fabric. Eventually she came to the section displaying a collection of more sophisticated designs. They were also more varied in their range of colors.

Suddenly she felt as if she were getting warmer, that things were heating up and that she was on the brink of discovering gold treasure, that the long hunt might finally be almost over.

She began carefully pulling out each gown so she could get a closer look at it. And then she saw it. It was unbelievably beautiful. As she gently took it out she caught her breath at how exquisite it looked and how perfectly it matched her vision.

It was a most mysterious color. Not quite gold, it had more of a pale bronze tint with a hint of blush mixed in. She wasn't quite sure that she had ever seen that exact shade before. The closest color she could compare it to was champagne. It was the most sumptuous champagne color she had ever seen, warmed considerably by hints of blush and bronze.

The under-dress was fashioned out of a damask textured fabric but of a very subtle, pale bronze color. The whole gown - bodice and skirt - was overlaid with a diaphanous champagne chiffon top dress in a barely visible, lyrical pale scroll pattern.

Hanging on the dressing room hook, it radiated a golden glow uniquely its own, delighting Helmi with its seductive allure. It seemed to be endowed with magical powers and she already felt wearing it was going to be one of the highlights of her wedding day.

Once she had picked out the perfect gown her mind wandered to thoughts of the honeymoon. Instinctively she sensed, deep inside, they were going to be the most enchanted days of her life.

She and Knute spent many magical moments envisioning how idyllic it would be to drive down the Coast Highway, lazing away their days in charming seaside inns. Together they relished imagining how they would go at a languid pace, spend lazy mornings sleeping in, have breakfast in bed, indulge in leisurely beach walks and devour decadent meals.

On the way home they wanted to circle around from the coast and explore the various vineyards and elaborate wineries scattered throughout the Hunt Valley. Then, heading north they would scour the Medina Valley and the Valley of the Moon, one of Jack London's favorite haunts. They were going to have to squeeze a great deal into a minimal amount of time in order to be back at Wildwood for the inaugural launching of their new product.

All the months leading up to the approaching wedding, they had devoted countless hours and expended every ounce of energy developing their precious equine healing balm. They finally decided to christen it Panasea of Gold, referring to its abundance of seaweed, the concoction's key curative ingredient. They eagerly anticipated an enthusiastic response yet remained only cautiously optimistic until they were actually up and running.

And so the countdown to their momentous day began. It finally dawned with a flourish on a gloriously golden morning. The garden soon swarmed into a maelstrom of activity. The florist, caterer and reception crew bustled about at their designated tasks.

Helmi watched as her vision of the rose-smothered arbor came into being. The minister's makeshift altar was set just inside where they would exchange their vows.

The musical combo arrived and began to practice softly in the background, their selections sounding vaguely fugue-like.

The reception tables were set up and the serving buffet assembled. Soon all was in readiness as the flower arrangements fell into place exquisitely.

Helmi scanned the scene one final time, seeing to it that it was to her satisfaction, then rushed off to her dressing room to don her gown for the five p.m. ceremony.

She could see, from her bay window, guests arriving, milling around, listening intently to the lovely strains of music and mingling among their friends.

Knute and Helmi had opted not to have attendants, to simplify matters. So now he waited, under the arbor with the minister, for Helmi to make her grand entrance.

Suddenly she appeared, utterly breathtaking, in her golden-bronze, chiffon gown. As she moved slowly toward him, Knute thought she seemed to float just beyond reach like a lovely shimmering mirage.

They breezed through a shortened version of the traditional nuptials. Immediately following the ceremony, they were quickly surrounded by admiring guests showering them with congratulations and warm embraces.

Soon silver trays laden with champagne-filled flutes were passed among the little throng of well-wishers. Next came trays of bite-size canapés.

The reception tent became a magnet for those in search of more substantial fare. Situated in the center of the Rose Garden, its interior was elegantly bedecked with table settings of luscious floral bouquets, lovely old linens and candelabras emitting a golden glow.

Above the hum of lively chatter, the strains of beautiful background music added greatly to the general ambience. But above all, every single diner seemed to purr with contentment, creating the room's unique sounding symphonic effect.

Dancing followed, lasting far into the wee hours of the night, until finally the brand new bride and groom slipped into the house to change into their going-away garb. Their absence was soon detected and the guests quickly lined two sides of the drive for the final sendoff.

When Knute and Helmi finally emerged everyone gasped at how radiantly passionate with love they looked. As they moved slowly along the reception line, shaking hands and accepting congratulations, a showering of apricot-colored rose petals rained down from above. Shrieking with delight they made a run for the getaway car and then they were gone.

Once they were out of the driveway and sufficiently far enough down the highway, Knute pulled off to the side of the road and removed the string of tin cans a practical joker at the party had tied to their bumper.

They smiled to each other a nod of tired relief, supremely happy just being alone together and finally setting out on their grand honeymoon adventure.

They decided to spend their first night in Aurora, a mere two hours south of the ranch.

By the time they arrived at their designated honeymoon hotel, the lovely old Villa Plaza, it was very late and they were thoroughly exhausted. So it was through sleepy eyes that they surveyed their luxuriously appointed suite which reignited their previous state of passionate excitement.

A bottle of champagne was chilling on the wood-paneled island's counter-top in the bar area.

A huge bouquet of white roses, lilies and peonies overflowed in a Chinese-patterned cachet pot encircled by lavishly upholstered living room furnishings. Every detail, much to their astonished delight, was fit for royalty, especially the deluxely proportioned bed which they eyed covetously. The view of the city lights from the sparkling wall of windows was magical.

Completely overwhelmed, they poured themselves tall glasses of champagne, raising them to clink the traditional celebratory toast. They were in the midst of what they surmised was every honeymoon couple's idea of newlywed heaven. All they wanted to do was snuggle together, cuddle down into the plush velvet sofa, and purr with contentment.

Reality soon crept in as they remembered the long drive ahead of them in the morning.

Helmi bounded up and headed for the dressing room alcove to slip into her filmy, buff chiffon negligee, while Knute explored the amenities in the sumptuous marble bath.

It was approaching five in the morning when they finally found each other in their monumental wedding bed. Neither had much left for anything more than a passionate goodnight kiss and they soon fell sound asleep.

Several hours later their room was already flooded with sunlight, waking them abruptly. It soon dawned on them that they had a long drive ahead and decided to order their breakfast from room service. By the time they were packed up it would be ready to be delivered.

Still in their night clothes they soon heard a knock on the door. Knute swung it open to let room service roll in their breakfast on a mahogany serving cart. It was a scrumptious array they surveyed.

The romantic notion hit each of them at the same time, that it was their first meal together as a married couple. The reception dinner had not really counted due to their excitement, causing a mutual lack of appetite.

The white-coated waiter lifted the silver covers off each dish revealing luscious looking Eggs Florentine-style omelets, freshly baked croissant rolls, bacon and strawberries smothered in whipped cream. There were pitchers, too, of freshly squeezed orange juice, French Roast coffee and Jasmine Blossom tea.

Suddenly they realized just how famished they felt and settled down to relish what seemed like one of the best breakfasts they had ever eaten.

Their long, leisurely feast soon refurbished their flagging energy reserves and they began preparing to depart.

As they stepped into the palatial shower stall together, their only wish was to have more time in which to savor those first shared moments of married magic.

Luckily, they reassured each other, they had the rest of their lives to make up for any time lost.

Quickly their thoughts fast forwarded to the road up ahead. They threw on the casual traveling clothes that they had previously laid out, then called the front desk to have their luggage taken down to the car while they checked out.

At last they were headed back down the coast on their way to the Hunt Valley. Along the way they reveled in the refreshingly pastoral sights on every side and around every turn. It was miles, hundreds of miles, of nourishing countryside, so restorative for their weary souls.

They knew they were in the vicinity not only by the balmy air and clear blue sky, but by row after row of cultivated grape vines. The precision of the symmetrically placed plants made them imagine they were watching a vast parade of military bands doing drills.

They could see in the distance, set atop a little knoll, the hazy silhouette of a majestic stone and stucco manor house. Its warm ochre façade had an inviting allure that intrigued them, compelling them to venture closer so they could explore it in depth.

As they arrived at the entrance drive, they were greeted by magnificent wrought iron gates ornately detailed and suspended from pillars of ancient brick. A welcoming sign to one side, fashioned out of wood and wrought iron and bordered by scrolls and vines announced they were entering the Domaine de la Contessa. From the moment they drove through the gates, a hushed spell fell over them conveying a sense of being on hallowed land. The atmosphere enveloping them eloquently confided that they were about to experience all the enchantments of an ultra exclusive gated estate.

The first sight that struck them simultaneously was how impeccably the vast property was manicured.

Clipped boxwood hedges hemmed in exuberant perennial flower beds planted in the cottage garden style. Intoxicatingly perfumed floral scents wafted over them from every direction. A swarm of exhilarated bumble bees, honey bees, birds, and butterflies hovered everywhere, industriously working their special territories.

And on the outskirts of all the lushness, as far as the eye could see, were rich green grapevines pendulously swagged with plump ripe grapes.

Just beyond the cultivated landscape, standing sentinel while providing both protection and privacy, towering cypresses stood casting shadows of mystery over everything that lay below.

Knute slowly eased the car up closer to the house and, noticing a sign stating Visitors' Parking, pulled into the designated spot. They then climbed a series of impressive stone steps. At the top they found the main entrance where they were met by two solid oak doors hand-carved with swags of vines, scrolls, and bunches of grapes. They were dark stained and so heavy that when Helmi tried to push them open, they slowly moved only a little bit at a time, seemingly reluctant to reveal what mysteries lay waiting within.

Stepping inside, through the darkness of the vast wood-paneled foyer, they saw an elegantly dressed and coiffed, middle-aged matron coming toward them with her hand outstretched hospitably.

"Welcome to the winery. May I introduce myself? I am Countess Francesca d'Amboise, the chatelaine," she said in a heavy French accent.

"We are Knute Corsun and my new bride, Helmi Seaborne," Knute responded in kind, instantly warming to the place.

"Follow me and I'll show you to the tasting room," she beckoned temptingly.

It didn't take much persuading for them to promptly comply.

She then led them down a dimly lit side hallway lined with elaborately gilded and shaded sconces.

The old iron hinges creaked as the countess pushed open the ancient carved wooden door, stepping aside to allow them to enter first.

The entire room was lined in clear cedar, even the ceiling, like a soothing spa and smelled of oak barrels and fruity wine. Against every wall stood tall pine wood shelves stacked with hundreds of cases of the estate's various vintage wines.

In an adjacent alcove, a heavy wood bar served as the tiny room's centerpiece and was stocked with bottles of wine across the counter top. A white-jacketed gentleman stood behind it.

"This is our tasting room and in charge of this part of our operation is our sommelier, Lucien," she told her captivated audience. "He will serve you some samples of our very best creations."

Lucien was already setting up two rows of ten sparkling wine glasses for each of them.

He started by pouring a pale white Sauvignon Blanc, watching intently as Knute and Helmi sipped rapturously. Then it was on through a succession of whites from a Chablis to a Chardonnay to a rare Pouilly Fume, all deepening into a rich, full-bodied golden shade.

It was then on to sipping a variety of reds, beginning with a light fruity Beaujolais, to a richer Merlot, Syrah, and the grand finale, a luscious Cabernet Sauvignon.

"We've received many honors and awards of distinction for our wines, but our special pride and joy is our brandy. Would you care to see the cellar where it is made?" she asked with an air of expectancy at the chance to show it off.

They vigorously nodded yes while quickly sneaking side glances at each other at their unexpected burst of good fortune.

"Come with me," she made a dramatic, sweeping motion with her arm, while leading them down a staircase of steep stone steps to the cellar.

Two imposing bronze-handled, wood-paneled doors opened into the brandy-making cellar. From the moment he stepped inside the cool, cave-like space, Knute was totally entranced. It embodied all the perfect elements of every type of mysterious atmosphere he had ever known and loved.

Row after row of wooden casks, stacked on top of each other, lined both sides of the narrow aisles.

"Here is where we distill the grape wine, in these oak casks, and where it is aged until maturity," the countess launched into her spiel about the brandy making process.

"The longer it remains in the casks the more it absorbs the tannins in the wood and takes on its tawny tint, which can be deepened even further by adding burnt sugar. Its strong bouquet comes from certain other alcoholic properties present. The high alcohol content is sometimes diluted with water by other distilleries, but we leave ours pure and untouched," she continued on with her clarification.

Knute and Helmi were beginning to feel much more enlightened about a substance that was rapidly becoming one of their favorite after dinner indulgences.

"This is an infinitely intriguing industry you're involved in," Knute effused, thoroughly impressed by all he was seeing and hearing. "How did you happen to acquire this estate and get into this business?"

"I'm originally from France. The ancestors of my late husband, Count Hubert d'Amboise, owned the Chateau d'Amboise in the Loire Valley for generations," she replied. "When we married he had already inherited the entire estate including a vineyard and wine-making operation.

"When he passed away, the overall scope of the enterprise turned out to be more than I could comfortably manage," she further elaborated.

"So I decided to sell, after much deliberation, and try my luck, with the proceeds, in this comparable area, only on a much reduced scale. Of course I brought a very knowledgeable staff with me from France, to whom I give much of the credit for our success," she concluded the shortened version of her saga.

"That is why this winery has a very French flavor about every aspect," she added as a final postscript.

"That's my favorite part," Helmi confided to her hostess. "That's what I love the most about it here, all the French touches and influences."

"It warms my heart, to hear you say that," the countess confessed. "It has been an extremely risky undertaking, but it finally seems to be paying off in more than a few ways. And I really do relish the opportunity of living in this glorious land."

As she spoke she led them over to an Old World-looking wet

bar area replete with an antique brass, shell-shaped sink and an onyx counter top and back-splash.

She took down two small cut-glass snifters from the overhead cabinet and poured brandy into them from a bottle of special reserve she had been saving for just such a moment.

"This is delicious," Knute raved as he inhaled, then took a sip of the precious amber-colored spirit.

"This is the best brandy I've ever had the good fortune to taste," Helmi echoed his exact sentiment at exactly the same time.

Countess Francesca flashed them her loveliest smile, obviously delighted by their shared responses.

"I'm pleased you are enjoying it so fully. It's the crème de la crème of our product line, one we relish sharing with our V.I.P. guests. If you warm the glass between the palms of your hands, its even more savory. That's why I gave you the smaller sized snifters. They're easier to caress that way," she instructed, arriving at the close of her tutorial on a most richly opulent note.

Their winery visit had been such an all-encompassing experience and had absorbed their attention so thoroughly that they had completely lost track of time.

Brought abruptly back to the present by the contessa's final flourish, they quickly realized that the afternoon was swiftly fleeting and there was still a great deal left for them to see and do.

It didn't take them long to decide to pick up where they left off the following day.

"We're so impressed with your ingenuity in pulling this place together," Knute told her," and by your entrepreneurial skills as well."

"Yours is truly an inspirational story," Helmi added, "one that we can carry home with us and put to use in our own special world. We're definitely indebted to you and so grateful to be the beneficiaries of your gracious and generous hospitality."

"It was every bit as enjoyable for me and fortunate, too, to have such attentive and appreciative guests as you two have been," she assured them.

"Unfortunately we really must be going," Helmi said, genuinely sorry at having to leave such exquisite surroundings. "We won't ever forget and hopefully, someday, might even be able to return."

"I'll look forward to that possibility," the countess answered, with equal regret at the romantic newlyweds' imminent departure. To her mind, they had been the best possible and most captive audience she could ever have hoped for.

And so it was with great reluctance they took their leave of the countess and headed back to the small country inn they had discovered to stay in while exploring the valley.

Along the way back they stopped in at several intriguing looking boutiques, a garden center, a bistro-style café, and even a prestigious riding stable.

By the time they arrived at the inn they were ravenous and went up to their charming room to change for dinner.

The meal was delectable, served in an authentically decorated French country style dining room. Each dish was prepared with the inn's own kitchen garden herbs, hand-picked vegetables, and only the freshest ingredients.

With every course, they were offered just the right local wine as a perfect accompaniment. It was a very romantic and enchanting ending to a very special day. It made them feel extremely fortunate, too, that, thus far, their honeymoon was sailing along so blissfully. Neither one of them could remember ever having had a more magical time in their lives.

Then it was off to bed to be ready for an early morning wake-up call. It was their plan, after breakfast in the inn's lovely palm courtyard, to head north to sample the winery offerings of the Medina Valley vineyards.

For the next several days they leisurely drove throughout the valley stopping frequently to sample the offerings of the various wineries. They felt great expectancy at every single vineyard, but none could match the Domaine de la Contessa's exquisite quality or even its inimitable hospitality. It was all a profound learning experience, as if they had attended an intensive wine-making seminar.

But they reluctantly came to the conclusion that it was time to head up the coast, back to Wildwood Ranch.

So the very next morning they packed up their things, loaded up the car and set off on their return voyage.

It was a lovely, scenic adventure, discovering unfamiliar sites along the rugged coastline on their journey home.

What they relished the most besides being within constant sight of the sea, was how much different all the flora and fauna surrounding them was from the usual they were used to seeing in their native region. All the plants and trees seemed so much more lush and exotic. And every bird and flower dazzled them with the sheer exuberance of their brightly colored petals, patterns, and markings. It was a naturalist's paradise and they felt privileged to be in the midst of such a vast expanse of unsurpassable wild beauty. To their overly activated imaginations, the only place that even remotely compared was their own tract of land running along beside the sea......

They were impatient to get home.

So instead of interrupting the flow of their return's momentum, they opted not to stay over anywhere, and pushed straight on back to the ranch.

At last they entered the welcoming approach road of their beloved Wildwood. Everything appeared just the same as they had left it seemingly ages ago, obviously well-tended during their absence.

Suddenly dumbstruck they stood bedazzled by Windflower's breathtaking beauty as she came running to them with all the graceful nobility of her ancient race.

The next few days they spent leisurely unpacking, generally settling in and slowly re-acclimating themselves to the familiar rhythm of ranch life.

Finally they found their way back to Windflower's side and to reacquainting themselves with the loving routine of her care. As before, it was a complex maintenance regimen that they never begrudged.

She was worth every precious moment of their time invested and every penny. They would forever consider her a priceless gift they had been granted, definitely worth her weight in gold.

It was a warm, sunny early fall day soon after their return. They decided to take a short hiatus and ride down to the beach.

Helmi saddled up Windflower and Knute leapt aboard the strikingly striped dun, his usual mount borrowed from the BLM's herd.

Horses and riders were rapidly rejuvenated once they hit their stride, trotting jubilantly alongside the sea.

It gave Knute and Helmi the perfect opportunity to further develop their production strategy, while simultaneously reveling in Windflower's remarkable recovery and recaptured enthusiasm for her seaside surrounding.

She was a joy to behold and reaffirmed their dedication to producing the miraculous balm that would create the same results for potentially millions of other creatures in need.

First on their wish list was creating a compelling package in which to place their product.

It had to be eye-catching enough to attract the masses, in a color that promised the contents capable of soothing as well as having the potential to completely cure.

After much vacillation and exploration they discovered a burnished bronze hue that appealed to both of them.

It was the exact shade of ageing seaweed, matching the mountains of it that were stored in their compost bin.

Then they moved on to selecting the shape of the container. They agreed that their precious balm would be enshrined in ceramic urn-like vessels. Each one would be stamped with a gold leaf horseshoe, the Wildwood Ranch logo.

Once their creation's outward look passed their scathing inspection and met their expectations enough to be presented to the outside world, they focused attention on the marketing campaign they referred to as the launch.

They had high hopes that their own beloved Panasea would generate the stir of excitement throughout the equestrian community needed for the dramatic introduction of a truly unique product.

So next they began to search for and recruit that rarest of commodities - a promoter skilled in handling newly patented, one-of-a-kind material.

They eventually found Cameron Gardner, whose impressive credentials matched their criteria amply. His inestimable worth, in Knute and Helmi's eyes, rested in his enthusiasm not only for their invention, but for the scope of their vision.

Instinctively he knew his first order of business was a media blitz - to infuse certain television, radio, newspaper, and magazine ads with pertinent information about the miraculous balm.

Even more specifically, he honed in on the innumerable equine periodicals, especially targeting specialized veterinarian journals.

Indefatigable, performing numerous advertising spots himself for both television and radio, he became the voice of Panasea and Wildwood Ranch. Soon it became known as Panasea Productions, leaving room for future expansion of the product line.

Helmi and Knute immediately picked up the pace of their output. They began stockpiling a massive supply of the balm in readiness for what they presciently foresaw would be a barrage of orders.

To insure that the assembly line continued humming and purring along as it had been, they hired two helpers.

And they were correct in their assumptions and optimism. Interest was keen even though, at first, new orders only came drifting in.

Little by little the trickle turned into a steady stream providing a healthy income to cover the hefty cost of the ranch's upkeep.

All those thousands of hours of backbreaking labor were beginning to be handsomely rewarded.

Slowly, as their visionary venture blossomed into a lucrative enterprise, the seed of the next pipe-dream began to germinate.

Veering onto a completely new path toward which their destinies were joined together, they harbored hopes of breeding Windflower.

Knute had long envisioned one of Windflower's foals as his own to ride instead of borrowing one from the BLM's herd, unique though it was.

And Helmi, deep in her heart, knew a filly or colt out of Windflower would not only be incredibly beautiful to behold but the beginning of a long line of special treasures to cherish forever.

It was a glorious Indian summer morning in mid autumn. They decided to sneak away from their regular routine, saddle up the horses and take them for a nature walk on the beach.

"What if we were to breed Windflower with this BLM stallion?" Knute posed the question to Helmi as they loped along the surf. "He would be the perfect sire with his unique heritage and striking markings and coloration."

"He most definitely is a handsome stallion with great conformation and musculature," she concurred. "But what is the history of his particular breed, do you know?"

"I've only picked up a few details from bits and pieces from the BLM. Supposedly it's descended from a rare band of wild horses that originate in a region somewhere around Mongolia. They all have the same characteristic striped legs, black dorsal stripe down the back and black mane and tail. They are usually dun-colored, the same body color that buckskins have.

"They were bred for endurance and toughness like the Appaloosa, in fact have a lot of the same ideal qualities as the Appaloosa. That's why certain Native American tribes have adopted it and carried on its lineage just as they have the Appaloosa line."

"It sounds like it would be a perfect fit for Windflower, a great combination of choice traits to intermingle," Helmi agreed wholeheartedly. "It looks like Windflower has finally met her match," she teased, eyeing Knute's charismatic stud.

And so, out of their fertile imaginings, the nucleus of a plan was born for their future breeding operation . And pivotal to their vision, still in only the pipe-dream phase, was the indispensable Windflower.

Her participation, with her impeccable bloodline and indomitable spirit, was essential in order for their dream to be brought successfully to fruition.

They were full of well-founded optimism as they watched their most recent venture, not only become a reality, but grow and flourish more every day.

As soon as they had formulated their breeding strategy, Knute began mapping out in his mind the look of the new barn that would house not only Windflower but her future progeny as well.

"It would have to have at least ten stalls," he said, immediately trying out his initial design ideas on Helmi, "and be built of cedar in the board and batten style."

"Go on," she prodded, amazed at such enthusiasm for yet another in a long line of many ambitious projects.

"We would want to have the space heated, lighted and water

piped in," he continued, "for drinking, bathing and cleaning."

"I think it would be nice to have a small office space that could also double as the tack room for the saddles, bridles and grooming gear," she added her suggestions to the growing wish list.

"Definitely," he quickly agreed, "besides a separate area to hold the bales of orchard grass and be right at our finger tips. It would make feeding time so much easier if we didn't have to keep going up and down to the hayloft.

"I think I'll be able to borrow Brice once in awhile from the BLM to assist in the raising of the frame. I can do most of the finish work myself, including splitting the shakes for putting on the roof," he summed up.

"I can picture exterior shutters on each side of the outside stall windows," Helmi elaborated on a few of her signature embellishments. "And, of course, a walkway overhang to keep the horses dry when it rains, besides adding significantly to the architectural style."

Knute was always the first to concur when it came to Helmi's suggestions regarding style.

"I'm already starting to feel like, architecturally, it's going to turn out to be a bona fide equestrian masterpiece."

"I'm feeling exactly the same way," Helmi admitted optimistically.

Shortly after the new barn brainstorming session, Knute began stockpiling building materials and leveling the land at the designated site.

From the beginning, from the foundation through the framing up, every phase of construction went quickly and smoothly.

Brice Selden came often from his work at the BLM to lend a hand with the heaviest jobs whenever summoned by Knute.

Slowly, as the new barn began to take shape, Knute and Brice started dismantling what remained of the old barn.

Part of it still sheltered Windflower, but most of what did still stand was only the charred remainder of one devastating night long ago.

Day by day, through all the changes, Knute and Helmi bore witness to the greatest change of all, Windflower's miraculous comeback.

Like a phoenix rising from the ashes, she metamorphosed into an heroic creature courageously mobilizing her inner forces to soar once again.

But her current metaphoric flight was nothing less than a winged victory. Unlike her previous escape, immediately following that terrible trauma, she was soaring away from those tragic moments toward survival's triumphant light.

Watching Windflower frolicking in the pasture, Helmi related to Knute sobering details of those first harrowing hours following the fire that she had not been able to reveal before.

Windflower had been literally out of her mind with pain and fear. She had escaped into a nether world of her own where she was all alone and no one could reach her. Initially she did not even recognize Helmi and would not allow her to come near. It had taken all of Helmi's patience and skill to lead her out of the barn and into the pasture.

Dr. Shelton, their vet, described to Helmi how it was like the human form of an hysterical fugue, a psychological phenomenon. It was a kind of amnesia brought on by some traumatic experience. He knew about it in people but, in all his years in practice, had never seen it surface in horses.

The more Knute heard, the more mortified he was, learning the extent to which Windflower had suffered. By the time he had returned she had rallied slightly and Helmi had chosen to spare him the worst while it was still so fresh and raw.

After everything she had been through it seemed inconceivable that they could be considering breeding Windflower or that she would ever be ready.

But daily they could see her gaining back her strength, gaining in self-confidence, regaining her spirit, and gradually improving on every level.

As the new barn neared completion, they were confident that Windflower would be perfectly poised to take on the new motherhood role.

In their leisure moments, they enjoyed imagining what her newborn would look like - its color, markings, conformation, sex, and whether it would be a colt or a filly. Either one would be welcome.

The barn, once finished, had a handsomely rugged exterior and surpassed their highest hopes.

The breeding facility was a well outfitted shed-like annex attached in back.

Helmi and Knute felt sure that Windflower and any of her offspring would be in horse heaven while in the warm, spacious, heated, straw-covered maternity stall.

It would be like staying in a luxurious, five-star hotel for horses with every necessity met and every wish fulfilled.

Breeding day arrived. Windflower pranced excitedly as if already sensing some new task up ahead that she would be lovingly expected to perform.

Always eager to please, she seemed patiently awaiting the challenge and perfectly willing to do her part.

Passionate horse lovers that they were, Knute and Helmi arranged for the long awaited mating to proceed as naturally as possible.

Knute brought his regular mount, the dun stallion, over from the BLM property and proceeded to reintroduce him to Windflower.

In the past they had been nothing more than saddle horses out for a ride, with no chance for romance.

But the proposed plan was to throw them together into a great grassy field where they would have little else but love to think about and ultimately be coaxed into coupling.

From that time forward it was primarily a game of waiting, wondering, and wishful thinking.

Secretly Helmi had always been inspired by Windflower in addition to her almost reverent admiration of her.

Since the day of their first meeting she was inspired by her proud, majestic beauty.

And witnessing her courage as she struggled through the terrible pain during the days after her first serious injury was profoundly inspirational.

Again the mare's indomitable spirit shone brightly through all the dark days of her long, slow comeback.

But, for Helmi, the lasting legacy of Windflower's greatness would forever be in knowing the extent to which she surmounted her suffering and the successful survival she so nobly gained after the tragic stable fire.

Helmi could only marvel at her current incarnation as a broodmare. In a certain way it eclipsed all of her previous impressive feats.

Windflower in foal, by some stroke of wizardry the thought of which held Helmi spellbound, surpassed every other inspired moment of the past.

It was the miracle of bringing another being into the world that, to Helmi, was infinitely inspirational.

The energy she drew from Windflower's endlessly inspiring example caused Helmi to search her soul as to her own priorities.

What she discovered was an intense desire to have a child, and one which would be the living testament to the enduring romantic love she had finally found with Knute.

It became, in her imagination, like a well-matched stakes race as to which of the two prospective mothers would conceive first.

Together and separately Knute and Helmi observed Windflower and the lusty stud from a discreet distance for signs of consummation.

As they predicted it was not long before their expectations were rewarded. They knew it may not be the first mating that would take, or even after many, that might result in a foal but ever the optimists they were extremely hopeful.

One late fall day Helmi ran to find Knute to spring her latest theory on him.

"It may just be a woman's intuition at work here," she burst out breathlessly, "but I think Windflower's pregnant."

"What makes you think so?" Knute calmly called for further clues.

"Well, we recently witnessed the stallion covering her. That's pretty strong support right there," she reminded him. "But aside from that she's acting oddly, and I've noticed how much she's been filling out lately."

"It all sounds promising," he agreed, trying not to get her hopes up just in case it was a false alarm. "But let's just wait and see a little longer and do some more close observing," he suggested sensibly, "before we call the vet to examine her."

Helmi, in her impatience, reluctantly agreed, knowing there

was no possible way she could control the course of nature.

With a great deal of delight all around, Dr. Shelton announced that Windflower was, indeed, in foal, confirming their hunches and bringing one more of their wild pipe-dreams to fruition.

The gestation period would take many months since the designated time for the foal's arrival was not until late summer or early fall.

They accepted the projected time frame with a sigh of relief, realizing it would give them the necessary breathing room to focus on widening the public's awareness of their new healing balm.

Dr. Shelton promised to be there for the foaling, great news for Knute and Helmi who took comfort in knowing they could rely on him and his experienced expertise at the much anticipated event. He assured them that their presence as well as participation would be welcome, which also overjoyed them.

So began their long vigil as they awaited the arrival of Windflower's foal.

Meanwhile, they continued developing the estate grounds, furthering production efficiency and distribution of Panasea, readying the barn for birthing and housing the new foal.

From the time they first realized Windflower was pregnant, the wet, windy months of her confinement flowed steadily along with routine ranch regularity.

Knute tended the various gardens, winterizing them against heavy frosts, flash floods and wild windstorms they battled annually.

Helmi had her designated areas as well including innumerable household chores, inside and out.

Together they tackled the stream of details inherent in their continuously expanding herbal enterprise, Panasea Productions.

But their hearts were most passionately involved with taking care of details concerning the well-being of the new foal. It had become their greatest priority.

Time passed quickly enough, being so fully packed with projects that it was.

Yet, conversely, the much anticipated event caused the hours, days and months to drag slowly along. It took every fiber of their beings to shore up their patience while remaining stalwart for the duration.

It was a warm, sunny day in late September and, remembering back, it was a day they would never forget.

Knute went to check on Windflower in the foaling stall. He found her lying on her side in the soft, clean straw, her belly fully exposed, huge and somewhat alarming.

At regular intervals she would let out a heart-wrenching groan. It was obvious that she was in the throes of labor and had been for some time.

He threw a blanket over her, gently rubbed her all over, cooed soothingly in an effort to comfort her and ran to find Helmi to convey the news.

She was hard at work in the processing plant preparing a new batch of balm.

"Windflower's colt is about to make his entrance," he announced with a note of pride, barely able to conceal his excitement.

"I've sensed, for quite awhile, that she was due any time," Helmi admitted. Immediately caught up in the magic of Knute's delightful news, she couldn't help ribbing him a little, "It sounds like you're pretty well convinced it's going to be a colt."

"Excuse the slip. It certainly wasn't intentional," Knute replied sheepishly. "Of course we'll welcome it whether it's a he or a she."

"I agree," Helmi concurred, "but I can see some of the advantages if it were to be a colt. For one thing, as a mature stallion it could become the cornerstone of our breeding stock. And how great for you to have a strapping stud as your kindred spirit kind of riding companion."

"So true," Knute noted. "Speaking of which, we'd better alert Dr. Shelton right away. We'll want him on hand for the foaling and he'll want to be there as much as we will."

"I'll go put in a call to him right now, letting him know it's urgent," Helmi volunteered, and headed off to use their direct line in the barn to notify the vet that Windflower's time had come.

Everything else was put on hold from then on as they tended to Windflower. Keeping her comfortable and tending to her needs were their foremost concerns of the moment.

So far she was holding her own bravely. They were also

acutely aware that she was looking heavily to them for their encouragement, support and the wealth of love and affection she'd grown accustomed to.

Finally Dr. Shelton arrived, hours later.

"I got your distress call," he explained, "but was in the middle of a very difficult case I'd been put in charge of."

Night had fallen, but inside the barn all was golden and glowing, warmed by the overhead floodlight streaming down from above.

He bent down on his knees to examine his favorite patient.

"Let's see how you're coming along, girl," he spoke to the most uncomfortable mare in a soft, soothing tone of voice.

"So, you're almost there. You'll have to give us some extra help," he told her. "You'll feel the urge, a huge pressure to push out with all your might."

Windflower nickered softly in response, as if to assure him of her cooperation.

"That's my girl," he patted her gently. "You're going to do just fine. Everything is looking just perfect."

He turned to Knute and Helmi, standing by to assist if needed, with his findings.

"She's fully dilated, which means it could be any minute now that the foal's head begins to emerge," he warned.

They could barely restrain their emotions, knowing it was one momentous occasion and one of the most moving they would ever witness.

Suddenly it began. They could see just a bit of cellophane-like film emerge, at first, the fetal membrane in which the foal was enshrouded.

Little by little more of the mysterious bag gushed out revealing the dark shadow of the form within.

Soon a tiny black nose poked through the misty veil and then two black front hooves attached to matchstick legs, then the tiny body and two more unfolding legs atop two black back hooves.

A final spurt of mucous-like blood expelled the last of the afterbirth and the delivery of the foal was complete.

The three onlookers were bathed in tears, realizing not only that the birth of every new life was a miracle but that Windflower's triumph over terrible odds to give life to this new colt was an even greater miracle.

"He's a fine specimen of a colt," Dr. Shelton proudly proclaimed. "He should be up and trying out those spindly new legs within half an hour or we'll have to give him a little nudge."

They watched the newborn's every minute movement, more enthralled with the charming spectacle than virtually anything else they had seen for a long time.

With that Windflower swung her head around toward the colt and gave him a gentle shove with her nose, encouraging him to get up.

Suppressed laughter came from the viewing threesome, subdued so as not to disturb the proceedings.

Slowly the leggy creature began trying to untangle the heap of limbs beneath him. As he struggled to stand, his wobbly legs resembled strands of wet noodles.

But they held him in place so that at last he was all the way up, if a bit shaky. His captive audience clapped and cheered their awe of his successful feat.

Finally they could see him all of a piece and sporting splendid markings. He was going to be a sublime stallion and would make a handsome sire, too, someday, they concurred unanimously.

Now we'll have to come up with a fitting name for him," observed Helmi, "one that captures his charisma."

That evening they dedicated to celebrating the new foal's entrance into their lives. Out came the silver champagne bucket, filled to the brim with sparkling cubes of ice.

Knute emerged from the newly-created cellar cradling a coveted bottle of La Grande Dame vintage Veuve Cliquot, chilled to perfection.

Helmi brought out the cherished gold-leaf accented, ribbed champagne flutes and the toasting began.

"Our long-time dream is finally fulfilled," Knute grinned, as he clinked glasses with Helmi, "and we're forever indebted to Windflower for it."

Tears spilled down Helmi's cheeks, mingling a myriad of mixed emotions, as she remembered the endlessly convoluted journey the three of them had traveled together.

"Thank heaven our colt is here at last, safe and sound with

us." Pausing she added slyly, "As a token of my inestimable appreciation for all you've been through with us, and for your infinite love and support, I wonder if you would do me the honor of accepting him as my heartfelt gift to you?"

Unable to find the words to respond to her generous gesture, he took the glass out of her hand, set it down, grasped her tightly to him and kissed her long and passionately.

That was all the thanks she needed, wishing this form of his overflowing gratitude would go on forever.

"Not only will you be able to give him the name of your choice," she went on after catching her breath," but train him in your own inimitable style. And when he's ready, we'll be able to ride the countryside together to our heart's desire."

"That is exactly the vision I have been entertaining in my own imagination. You must be clairvoyant," he replied with obvious esteem.

And, refilling their glasses, they drank another toast, this time with even greater zeal than the first.

From then on, they kept a close watch on the little foal's progress with ever increasing relish.

They were captivated by his antics, observing him snuggle up to his mother while nursing and the delight with which he was discovering all the newness surrounding him.

They particularly cherished seeing him flourish daily as he slowly began to fill out, thriving on his mother's loving ministrations and in every other possible way.

One crisp, late fall day Knute was at his usual lookout, watching his still nameless colt when suddenly an idea flitted into his thoughts.

How starry-eyed his gaze is. That's it. That's what I've been waiting for. Finally his name makes a grand entrance onto the stage of my mind and its all lighted up as if on a billboard. I'll call him Stargazer. It suits him perfectly. Not only is it the name of an Oriental lily, one of our favorite garden flowers, but it befits his most prominent characteristic,

which is that of a dreamer, beyond all
daydreamers, the strongest of all
bonds between us.

Armed with this latest revelation, he went to find Helmi to tell her of his epiphany and hear her response, for or against.

"It's an absolutely exquisite match," she exclaimed enthusiastically, "so befitting the demeanor of our entrancing dreamer."

"I was hoping you would see it that way," Knute preened, puffing up like a peacock at his stroke of sheer genius. "It's settled then. From now on, the world will know Windflower's progeny as Stargazer. I think she will be wild about how well it encapsulates his lyrical spirit.

Not long after that momentous day, Knute and Helmi were out at the barn reveling in the sight they beheld.

Windflower and Stargazer were standing side by side in adjacent stalls of their spacious new quarters.

It was a special shared moment of deep meaning to them both and a long held dream realized.

Helmi was overcome with emotion. Tears of joy and gratitude, for Windflower, for Stargazer, for Knute, streamed down her cheeks.

"There's something I've been meaning to tell you," she began hesitantly, as if not knowing exactly the best way to proceed.

Knute knew that tone in her voice, that something significant was up ahead.

"Windflower's saga, up to and including the fulfillment of motherhood, has, from the beginning, been profoundly inspirational to me," she professed, unmasking her inmost sentiments to Knute.

"Her tenacity in achieving her maternal destiny has instilled the same desire in me. That is why I am so proud to be able to share my secret that I've been saving for just such an occasion. I am carrying our child. We, too, are going to be parents."

Knute had harbored the possibility, but, with his suspicions confirmed, he was far more emotionally moved than he ever imagined he would be now that the news had actually come.

With the advent of Stargazer and now, knowing he was

going to be a father to his own son or daughter, he was tremendously touched.

Tears of wonder welled up in his eyes as he beheld Helmi as if for the first time, the vessel within which resided their precious, jointly-created treasure.

Later that afternoon, walking back to the house, Helmi stopped and turned to Knute as if she'd just been struck by a sudden revelation.

"You know, it seems to me there's another very important reason why this colt should be called Stargazer."

"Yes? What is it?" Knute's piqued curiosity urged her to continue.

"Well, it's just this," she went on, taking the cue from his gentle prod.

"Stargazer is such a fitting name precisely because he is, and forever will be, our star. Windflower and Stargazer are the twin stars of Wildwood Ranch."

"I couldn't have put it better myself," Knute concurred. "I agree one hundred per cent with your very astute summation, which is also a very profound truth."

And, arm and arm, they continued strolling leisurely back to the house to celebrate the surprising new developments within their normally tranquil domain.

"A toast to the newest members of our tribe," Knute saluted, gingerly stroking Helmi's burgeoning belly. "And a toast to the indomitable, the irrepressible, the invincible Windflower, who has always faced unimaginable adversity with courage, style and grace."

"And," Helmi chimed in, echoing his fierce devotion, "no matter how daunting her travails, her intrepid spirit, like a phoenix literally rising from the ashes, continues to soar over every obstacle put in her path and through it all her heart continues to sing."

Festively clinking glasses, they each had a golden, glowing vision of Windflower gloriously cloaked in her lilting, soaring spirit, careening, like the Winged Victory, down the last stretch of life's final furlong, crossing over the finish line triumphantly.

THE END

ABOUT THE AUTHOR

Martha Lee

Martha Lee, artist and writer is a Washington state native born in Chehalis, Washington. She now lives on a small ranch in Ocean Park, WA on the Long Beach peninsula with her Appaloosa horse, Gypsy.

She has worked as a reporter for the Seattle Post-Intelligencer and has written short stories and has completed two novels. Her poetry chapbook, To the Beach and Other Poems has been published in two editions, the first having her original artwork for its covers.

An artist as well, she has painted, professionally, in oil on canvas for over thirty years. Her paintings are represented in private and public collections throughout the United States including collections in Washington D.C. Her work is available through marthaleestudio.com.

A biographical profile of her has recently been selected for inclusion in the 68th Edition of Marquis' *Who's Who in America, 2014.*

Made in the USA
Charleston, SC
07 September 2013